CALM THE STORM

Society of Swans
Book 2

Penny Fairbanks

ARE YOU SIGNED UP FOR DRAGONBLADE'S BLOG?

You'll get the latest news and information on exclusive giveaways, exclusive excerpts, coming releases, sales, free books, cover reveals and more.

Check out our complete list of authors, too!

No spam, no junk. That's a promise!

Sign Up Here

www.dragonbladepublishing.com

Dearest Reader;

Thank you for your support of a small press. At Dragonblade Publishing, we strive to bring you the highest quality Historical Romance from some of the best authors in the business. Without your support, there is no 'us', so we sincerely hope you adore these stories and find some new favorite authors along the way.

Happy Reading!

CEO, Dragonblade Publishing

**Additional Dragonblade books by
Author Penny Fairbanks**

Society of Swans Series
Awaken the Heart (Book 1)
Calm the Storm (Book 2)

CHAPTER ONE

July 1811

Y AWNING ALOUD, FELICITY rubbed sleep from her eyes as she slumped into her usual chair. Across the breakfast table, Mercy wrinkled her nose before turning her attention to the selection of cold meats and breads presented on gleaming, silver platters. Her graceful fingers fluttered in the air, a sign of careful deliberation.

"Good morning, sister," Mercy said, clearing her throat.

"Morning, it is. 'Good' is still to be determined," Felicity grumbled in return, a few droplets of hot chocolate splashing onto the dangling sleeve of her green morning robe thanks to her careless pouring.

Mercy lifted a brow but remained silent. *"You brought that upon yourself with your haste,"* the look said.

Felicity rolled her eyes and disappeared behind her cup, taking a long, deliberate sip of her favorite bittersweet beverage. She made a note to herself to arrange an apology gift for her poor lady's maid for yet another stained garment in a week of particular absentmindedness. Not that the cheery Hammond expected anything less from her young mistress after dutifully serving the older Reeve twin since their debuts five years prior. Felicity had never been one to hide her tendency to find herself in messes. She let out a loudly satisfied sigh and smacked her lips for added effect.

Early morning sunlight filtered in through the tall windows on the adjacent wall. It turned the blonde curls framing Mercy's face under her nightcap into perfect, golden ringlets as she ignored Felicity's antics. She was Felicity's mirror, identical down to the detail, and had fought her way into the world on Felicity's heels. They were both highly stubborn and independent.

Yet despite the superficial similarities between the Reeve twins, Mercy had always favored propriety, whereas Felicity could not care less. Why should she have to care in their own home, in their own breakfast room, especially when they took almost all their meals alone, save for planned luncheons or dinner parties? There were no guests or parents to impress.

It was always just Felicity and Mercy.

"Have you any plans for the day?" Mercy prompted as she buttered her toast with sharp, precise swishes.

Felicity set her cup down on its saucer, plucked up her fork, and stabbed a slice of cold ham. "Goodness, I shall have to consult my schedule. It is positively brimming with engagements, you see," she announced with a delighted grin before taking a generous bite.

The other lady shook her head and laughed. "If you insist, but should you find the strength to wrest yourself away from your riveting, imaginary schemes, you are more than welcome to join me on a walk to the village in the afternoon."

"Why must you be so tiresome and inquire after my plans if you knew quite well that I had none? You wound my delicate pride!" Felicity teased, fanning herself with one hand as if on the verge of a fainting spell, the drama in her expression giving way to a smile.

"I do pity you, poor creature!" Mercy let her toast fall to the plate and pressed both hands to her chest, clutching at her frilly nightgown.

The sisters' laughter echoed through the breakfast room, exquisitely appointed in their mother's taste yet devoid of warmth, much like the woman herself. Mercy could never resist her twin's silliness for long when in the privacy of each other's company, which was often when within the walls of Huxley Manor.

"I must confess this past week in Bainbridge has brought an unexpected change upon me." Felicity gasped as their mirth died away and a rumble seized her mostly empty stomach.

"Indeed?" Mercy asked, watching Felicity over the rim of her teacup. "You have seemed in quite a daze recently."

Felicity pursed her lips and glanced down into the chocolatey depths of her drink. She shared *everything* with her twin, her dearest confidant even amongst their circle of lifelong Bainbridge friends who were near enough to be considered sisters themselves. That did not mean Felicity was always free of embarrassment just because she and Mercy had met in the womb.

"Being home in the country has been exactly what I need," Felicity confessed in a rush, keeping her eyes down to avoid Mercy's ever-curious and observant study. "Calm and quiet."

Even without looking up, Felicity could feel her sister's brows rise. Felicity snatched her fork and prodded at the lumps of cheese and bits of bread she'd haphazardly piled onto her plate, feigning a sudden yet immense interest in organizing her food.

"Well, good for you for recognizing what you need."

From the corner of her eye, Felicity could see Mercy nod firmly and bring her fists, closed loosely around utensils, down to the table with a decided *thud*. The younger twin's silverware clattered softly against her plate as she set them aside and folded her hands in her lap, attention fully on the elder.

Suppressing a groan, Felicity sat back against her chair and slid down, desperate to free herself of this unwanted scrutiny. The expression of feelings had never been one of her natural gifts—not like her sister, who could summarize her every emotion into a few artfully succinct words. No amount of consideration in Felicity's mind could ever produce any meaningful reflection of her feelings. Thus, she did not often bother to try.

"You *are* normally eager to return to the bustle and excitement of London by now..." Mercy allowed her voice to trail away, offering an invitation to Felicity, a hand to guide her in the right direction.

Felicity shrugged, an action that would have had their mother, Lady Eldmar, fanning herself in fury at such undignified behavior from a viscount's daughter, even in the security of their own walls.

"I suppose, after the events of last Season, I am happy to have some time to breathe and collect myself," she mumbled, worrying at the embroidered edge of her napkin. "Especially since Mother has been preoccupied with making our return known to her Bainbridge friends."

Mercy took a deep inhale and closed her eyes, her own weariness evident in her bowed head. "The woman has been relentless," she hissed between clenched teeth. "At one point in my life, I thought I would like to have her notice, but I would vastly prefer her neglect to this recent parade of events and potential suitors that is beginning to feel endless."

The twins agreed on all points about their mother—about both their parents—but one. Mercy had once longed for their love and care, outgrowing the desire over time. Felicity had never desired it at all. Why should she waste her heart on wanting anyone who did not want her?

"I cannot blame you for seeking rest, dear Felicity," Mercy continued. "Though I do not disdain country quietude as much as you do, I have also found myself in particular need of Bainbridge's peace." She took a long sip of tea, closing her eyes and tilting her head back.

Felicity nodded her agreement with both Mercy's words and her unspoken appreciation of her drink. Somehow, even the tea tasted better, had a greater calming effect here than it did in London. Especially after such a whirlwind of a Season, which had culminated in the joyful marriage of one of their best friends, produced by rather unusual circumstances.

Felicity's nod quickly turned to a shake, soft ringlets brushing against high cheekbones, banishing those thoughts that tiptoed toward the thing she least wished to dwell upon: mysterious matches and their makers. She rather felt she had had enough of that nonsense to last a lifetime.

And she had not even been the target of that bizarre matchmaking scheme! Stoic Miss Lydia Dailey had borne her role with the perfect dignity their friends had come to expect of the group's eldest and leader. Now she reaped the reward as Mrs. Harrowsmith, married to her oldest and dearest friend, Sebastian. At least Lydia had longed for such a happily ever after.

As long as certain anonymous writers recognized that some women abhorred the institution of marriage and kept Felicity out of her sights, she could enjoy her respite in the country, pray that Lady Eldmar would give up her zealous attempts to send her youngest two children down the aisle, and return to London refreshed and full of vigor for the exhilarating variety of pursuits only available to a young lady in such a city.

"Trust that I do not say this lightly," Felicity began with a commiserating smile. She took up her fork once more, eager to leave the subject behind entirely. "But I believe several quiet months in the country is just what we need. Even Mother cannot make potential husbands appear for us out here, at least not any whom we have not already scared away."

The sisters laughed once more, Felicity's relief reflected in her twin's bright-brown eyes. The breakfast room door creaked open and all sound ceased.

"The morning post, misses," a footman announced as he marched inside, holding out a small, silver tray with one graceful arm.

Felicity grasped the neat stack of letters. "Thank you, Isaac."

The door clicked closed behind the servant and Felicity's fingers danced across the deliveries. "For you. For you. Also for you," she mumbled listlessly, dropping each one in turn onto

Mercy's outstretched, expectant hand. "And one for me."

Leaning back in her chair, Felicity held her only note in one hand and enjoyed another sip of chocolate. Not an unusual distribution for the morning post, nor did Felicity mind. She was a terrible correspondent. The process of writing out her comings and goings and her thoughts on them was far too odious to engage her attention for long. Besides, anyone worth sharing such things with lived a mere walk away and would hear it all from her mouth directly.

More interested in her chocolate than the letter, Felicity indulged in another sip as she glanced over her name on the front, written in patient flourishes and swoops. She flipped the letter over. Her eyes went directly to the wax seal.

A swan in deep purple. The lukewarm liquid curdled in Felicity's throat. She sputtered and managed to swallow, flicking the single small sheet onto the table as if it had scalded her.

"Felicity!"

Mercy shot to her feet, the discordant scraping of her chair against the wooden floor echoing in Felicity's ears. Everything felt both too distant and too close all at once.

Felicity could only force her bulging eyes up to meet Mercy's concerned stare. It was enough to convey all the information her twin needed.

CHAPTER TWO

"*D*EAREST MISS REEVE, *I trust that my letter finds you only mildly surprised, given the events of last Season. If you are indeed reading these words, that means your curiosity has won out over your disdain for all things related to matrimony—which, unfortunately, dominates most of a woman's life from the moment of her birth.*

"*On that, I shall not disagree with you. But by opening this letter, you show that deep within your heart, there lies hope, no matter how small. Even if you roll your eyes or scoff at the very notion—*"

Clara paused and sucked in a deep breath through plump lips, all attention on Felicity as she caught herself in the middle of a gratuitous roll of the eyes. Growling under her breath, Felicity slammed her eyes shut and turned her back on her sister and their four friends, perched on iron chairs protected by the shade of the large, white pavilion nestled in the heart of Huxley Manor's lavish gardens. Not one had yet touched their tea.

"Continue, Clara," Lydia prodded, nodding to the youngest of their group and their best orator. The newly married lady returned her sharp, blue eyes to Felicity's pacing form, thundering up and down the row of hedges leading to the pavilion.

Filling her rosy cheeks with air once more, Clara found her place in Lady Swan's letter. "*Even if you roll your eyes or scoff at the very notion, perhaps there is something inside you that longs to know if it might be possible. If you, Miss Felicity Reeve, might be worthy of embarking upon the most mysterious and thrilling adventure of all: love.*

"*Open yourself to more changes in your world and your heart.*

Perhaps you have lived in one cage so long, you now only see traps around every corner—and an unknown cage could always be worse than the old.

"If you open yourself to one thing, let it be this: A new arrival may offer a new perspective.

"Last but most certainly not least, never forget that you deserve to walk your own path of happiness, and the right gentleman will gladly walk it by your side as a partner, as a half that brings wholeness and shines the brighter for your presence.

"Your most loyal servant, Lady Swan."

Clara's voice faded on the warm breeze. The ladies in the pavilion looked at each other in awed silence. Felicity continued to kick up dust and bits of gravel with her walking boots as she stomped back and forth along the path, lavender skirts fluttering about her ankles.

All at once, the group burst into chatter, questions, speculation, and accusations flying through the air. Felicity clenched her teeth to drown out the noise, rather more familiar with being the *cause* of it than its victim.

Had summoning all their friends to inspect the letter really been the best idea? Of course Mercy had insisted. Lydia had done the same when she had received her letter. They were bound together by this mystery, this anonymous matchmaker who possessed uncanny, almost personal knowledge. Especially now that the mystery was no longer confined to just one Season, to just Lydia and her now-husband, Sebastian.

But why, why, why, Felicity thought to herself, each word punctuated by an irritated stomp, *did it have to be* her? Surely, given everything Lady Swan apparently knew, she would know that this was the last thing Felicity wanted.

It must have been a joke. A prank. That was what Lydia had originally thought, though in her situation, the letters had proven genuine. And if it was not a prank, if this Lady Swan truly thought she could find just the man to tempt Felicity, well, Felicity was no stranger to disappointing others.

"Wait a moment!" Isabel's voice cut above the clamor. She

stood in the center of the pavilion. The black curls peeking out from beneath her bonnet bounced as she looked from Clara and Lydia on one side to Mercy and quiet, wide-eyed Ellen on the other.

"We could be revealing valuable information, but no one will hear it because we are all speaking over each other," she continued in her usual studious tone, index finger jabbed smartly into the air. "Speak one at a time, please. Now, the only vacant house I am aware of in the area is Setherwell Court, so perhaps this new arrival means to take it. Has anyone heard of any gentlemen or families coming in to let the place?"

"Well, one of the shopkeepers in the village mentioned to me the other day that a handsomely wealthy gentleman is looking to take a house," Clara began, doll-like features aglow, complemented by a lovely, blush dress.

Felicity's stomach twisted. She crossed her arms tightly across her chest, fingers digging into the flesh of her arms. Surely, the mystery could not be solved already. Lady Swan had made it too easy last time, though they had found their own ways to overcomplicate matters.

"But," the younger Gardiner sister continued, her ever-optimistic smile fading, "the gentleman, now out of mourning for his late wife, is looking for a house in Frampton, near where his grandson and new great-grandchild live."

"Be sure that shopkeeper does not let our mother hear any such thing," Mercy said through gritted teeth, crushing a napkin in her fist. "The viscountess might prove desperate enough to seriously consider marrying one of us off to a great-grandfather."

A shudder rippled through the gathering of young ladies.

"I am sure Lady Swan does not intend on *that*," offered Ellen, the shyest and sweetest of their group. She nervously cradled a gold inlay porcelain teacup in both petite hands, her gaze a warm, deep brown. "No doubt we will hear something of new residents any day now," she finished with a cautiously hopeful smile.

Isabel hummed, frowned, and grasped a shallowly dimpled

chin with lace-covered fingers. Just as her lips parted to deliver some futile theory or other, Felicity rounded on the pavilion.

"Do not bother wasting your time or breath," she barked, chest heaving with her increasing frustration, eyes ablaze.

"But dear Felicity—"

"If it worked for Lydia—"

"—a blessing in disguise!"

"—have yet to consider—"

"I, for one, am not surprised by my sister's reaction," Mercy called over the rising racket. She shot Felicity a smile that conveyed both apology and commiseration before turning her gaze to the others. "Do you all truly expect Felicity to skip to the altar simply because Lady Swan says it must be so?"

Always the picture of perfect manners, Lydia pursed her lips as she neatly folded her napkin with practiced dexterity and placed it on the small table she shared with Clara. Leaning forward, she fixed Felicity with a pensive, blue stare. "Are you still so ardently opposed to marriage after everything you witnessed these past few months?"

Felicity suppressed the urge to roll her eyes, now entirely too conscious of her frequent reliance on the expression thanks to Lady Swan. Instead, she shook her head. The maddening energy that made her every limb itch with the need for movement required release in some form.

"Of course you must have had a change of heart, Felicity, haven't you?" Clara sat up taller in her chair and clasped her hands together under her chin expectantly.

Heaving a sigh, Felicity rubbed at her temples. "I am thrilled for you, Lydia, I truly am. And I am hopeful for everyone else's prospects. But none of that changes my knowledge that marriage would be nothing short of a prison for someone like me."

"But—"

"I simply will not suffer any man to crush me into a meek, simpering wife whose only concern is maintaining the family's appearances," Felicity snapped. Shame tinged her cheeks when she saw Clara shrinking away from the harsh interruption. She quickly lowered her head in a silent apology.

"But..."

Every head turned to the source of that soft word. Poor Ellen, frightened even of her own shadow, stared squarely at Felicity. The older Gardiner sister's countenance was so earnest that Felicity could not help allowing her stubborn resistance to deflate. Just a little, just for the member of their circle who held the tenderest spot in each of their hearts. She waved a limp hand through the air.

"But that is not what happened to Lydia and Sebastian," Ellen continued, glancing across the pavilion to Lady Swan's most recent success.

Felicity huffed and pouted, turning to face the nearest hedge. Her gloved fingers played over the sturdy, green leaves like pianoforte keys and her eyes traced warped shapes created by the hollows of neatly trimmed branches.

The feeling of so many fascinated eyes fixed so firmly in her direction for once did not suit her. Not when she could feel the unwanted tug of true emotion building in her throat. She knew her friends knew, but they did not *understand*—because Felicity had never allowed them to.

Their silence and expectation weighed on her narrow shoulders. She took a steadying inhale and pinched a leaf between forefinger and thumb, plucking it.

"The Harrowsmiths are the exception rather than the rule, based on my observations of my parents and older brothers and sisters. None of them love their spouses because none of them have anything in common. I know the only love my parents share is a love of ostentatious glamor and the finest connections their rank can buy."

Felicity flicked the leaf away, following it with her eyes as it trailed to the grass below so as not to catch glimpses at her friends' no doubt pitying expressions. Her hatred of the sharing of her intimate thoughts and pains came second only to her hatred of marriage.

"Indeed…" Isabel mumbled. Heat rippled up the back of Felicity's exposed neck, aided by the powerful midday sun above, at the unnecessary melancholy in her friend's tone. "Given that, I can see why you do not hold a high opinion of the supposed benefits of marriage when you have only seen the flaws that cannot be exposed until after it is too late."

"I do not believe Lady Swan is advocating for poor matches made in haste with only material or social advantage in mind," Lydia added slowly.

"She might be, if Lady Swan's true identity is Mrs. Cullham, as you seem to think, Lydia," Isabel said, wrinkling her nose. "That old gossip would throw any young lady at any single man, no matter how unsuitable, merely for her own entertainment. Still, Lady Swan or not, I am sure she already knows who is coming to Bainbridge. She has her ways of ensuring her ears are the first to hear, as old gossips do."

"Impossible!" Clara cried, stomping one slippered foot. "Lady Swan writes with such thoughtfulness and kindness. Have any of you ever heard Mrs. Cullham say anything even remotely resembling thoughtful or kind to or about anyone?"

"Clara, watch your tongue!" came Ellen's inevitable response.

A few moments later, Felicity's companions had once again devolved into overlapping discussion of encouragements and theories—none of which involved the writer herself. Apparently, as far as the girls were concerned, now that Lady Swan's methods had been proven, there was no longer any need to discern her identity as well.

The sound of their mingling voices, normally so welcome, grated against her nerves like silverware against china, building into a nearly unbearable thumping pressure between her ears. Felicity lowered her head and grabbed a fistful of shrubbery.

She did not like this feeling of everyone *caring* so much about her. About her future. She would rather they care about her foolish behavior or unrefined manners. Felicity stretched her neck from side to side, eager for relief.

Lord and Lady Eldmar certainly had not cared about anything Felicity and Mercy did or did not do until last year, when local gossips had taken up the virtuous cause of speculating that the viscountess was failing her youngest daughters by not putting forth more effort into marrying them off.

If there was one thing their mother could not abide, it was a less-than-sparkling reputation to match those of her equally brilliant friends. Thus had begun Lady Eldmar's crazed mission to throw the twins at as many eligible men as possible during the Season.

Felicity's tensed muscles began to ache and tremble with the effort of remaining still, containing her simmering exasperation and resentment. Now, thanks to Lady Swan poking about in Felicity's business, even her friends—who had always understood and accepted her—sought to take charge of her life.

"Here, I know just the thing!" Isabel once again threw her full voice across the pavilion. "Why don't we read the letter again from the start and examine it, line by—"

Enough!

The last thread of sanity clinging for dear life finally snapped. Felicity's eyes flew open, chest heaving, sweat beading at the nape of her neck. Digging her heels into the gravel, she spun sharply and marched.

"Wait!"

"I told you not to—"

"Felicity, please!"

"No, no, friends. I am sorry, but I believe my sister requires some time and privacy."

"Oh, dear…"

The voices of Felicity's companions faded quickly, whisked away by a stiff, summer gust. Her field of vision narrowed to the end of the hedge row straight ahead and the expanse of cornflower-blue sky beyond, skirts snapping around her legs with the briskness of her pace.

Felicity fought to keep every breath measured, to keep her walking boots firmly on the earth, as she stormed across the imposing shadow of the home that had polished generations of Reeves and through the stunning gardens personally curated by the current viscountess herself.

Her footsteps hastened into a half-run the moment her eyes caught sight of that familiar break in the thin copse. In truth, it was more of an impression between the trees. That dreadful, suffocating lump growing in her chest urged Felicity forward. The delusional promise thudded with every pained heartbeat that as soon as she left Huxley Manor and its inhabitants and guests behind, she could breathe once more. She would be free.

Branches snagged at Felicity's dress as she pushed in, leaves whispering across the exposed skin of her upper arms and neck. A moment and a nearly twisted ankle later, she burst through the other side onto a cobbled street. Felicity glanced up and down the small, shaded path that served her home as well as Isabel's to the left and to her right, the only unoccupied estate in Bainbridge.

Turning, she broke into a full run—at least as full as her lady-like walking boots and layers of pale-purple skirts would allow. Her poor bonnet fluttered against the strong wind flying into Felicity's face. She did not care if the blasted thing should be carried off amongst the stars. She had a dozen more just like it, and another dozen even finer. Besides, Felicity had always found bonnets to be cumbersome at best and a bane at worst during the times one longed to feel the sun warming one's hair and the fresh air on one's cheeks.

She continued to run, arms pumping, a smile forcing its way onto her lips. This moment of freedom felt too good for her to be wrong. Felicity would prove to herself that it was Lady Swan who was incorrect. Whatever triumphs the matchmaker had claimed in the past, Felicity was determined not to number among them in the future.

No one knew Felicity better than herself. No one was coming to sweep her off her feet.

If they tried, she would simply continue running.

At the curve in the path up ahead, obscured by the overhanging trees lining the street, Felicity's wondrously burning lungs squeezed shut. Her eyes widened. She skidded to a halt as an exceedingly handsome, silver-painted, dark-wood coach turned down the drive of Setherwell Court, a smaller cart bearing luggage behind it.

"Impossible," Felicity half-whispered, half-wheezed. One hand pressed against her hammering heart, the other covering her open mouth.

Could Lady Swan predict the future? Or perhaps she had merely heard the rumors and thought to apply her knowledge to the entertaining activity of sending young ladies on quests for their roles in fabled love stories.

Astonishment gave way to curiosity. Waiting until the luggage cart passed under the grand, stone archway, Felicity seized the first opportunity to duck behind the tall, spiral-shaped hedges that lined the drive and followed along. As she crouched behind the nearest hedge possible, a most undignified position, Felicity prayed they had simply taken a wrong turn or were passing through and thought to have a glance at an available house.

She hissed when the driver pulled through the loop at the foot of the front steps and slowed the horses to a stop. Even from this distance, Felicity noted the beautiful dress of the older couple that stepped down from the carriage.

The more she saw, the deeper Felicity's heart sank. A butler, who had apparently been sent ahead, hurried down the steps and familiarly greeted the lady and gentleman, who must be his master and mistress. So they were prepared to stay.

A muscle twitched in Felicity's jaw. Even worse, everything in their possession and every aspect of their air indicated nothing short of a splendid fortune. They must have had one, if they sought to take Setherwell Court, often said to be the finest property in Bainbridge after the Reeve family's.

The man and woman followed their butler up the steps, he

with a puffed chest of admiration and she with a sparkling smile of satisfaction. The carriage door opened again, foiling Felicity's feeble hopes that instead of a tempting bachelor, Bainbridge had gained nothing more than another mature couple with children already settled.

A hunched figure squeezed into the modest doorframe. The gentleman's face was obscured by a book, one long leg reaching for the ground, bypassing the single step.

Bells of alarm trumpeted in Felicity's mind. Her eyes felt as though they would pop from her head with her desperation— mingled with a not-insignificant portion of horror—to see more of this particular stranger.

He took one step out of the carriage. With her eyes as fixed on him as they were, it was impossible for Felicity not to witness the man's other foot catch on the carriage interior.

"Gah!"

He stumbled, his clearly fascinating book dropping to the gravel in a little cloud of dust, revealing a young profile with a slightly hooked nose and a mouth given to panicked muttering. The stranger removed his top hat and tucked it under his arm as he collected his book. With hasty care, the gentleman brushed the debris from the front and back covers and brought it closer to his face, examining its every detail.

The older couple paused at the top of the stairs, glancing over their shoulders. Unconcerned by the bumbling fellow down below, they disappeared into the shadowy foyer.

The younger man still stood in profile as his chest filled and deflated quickly in what appeared to be a good-natured chuckle. He shook his head. Dark-brown hair, still tousled from the hat, fell in thick, straight pieces across his eyes. Too far for Felicity to make out their color. An irrelevant detail, in any case.

Before she could identify the strangely airy feeling in her chest, a quiet laugh spilled from Felicity's lips. In all of a minute or two, she had surmised that this must be a frequent occurrence for the gentleman. The couple, most likely his parents, had been completely unperturbed. He, once assured of his book's safety, had been merely amused.

What an absurd idea! Who on Earth could love reading so much, they refused to lift their nose from the pages long enough to guarantee their safe exit from a carriage?

Surely not. Surely, Lady Swan did not think this scholarly type would suit Felicity. A shiver shot down Felicity's spine at the thought. She shook her head to banish the absurd notion and returned her gaze to the house.

The man had turned. He was staring in her direction.

Heart shooting into her throat, Felicity yanked herself behind the full coverage of the spiral hedge, back pressed against neatly trimmed leaves. His sweeping gaze had nearly caught her.

What *had* caught her was the unexpected full view of his countenance. She had not thought he would be *that* handsome.

Or was it that thoughtfully curious expression, all furrowed brows and pouting frown, as he searched for whatever or whoever had made the sound—as he searched for *her*—that had somehow blinded Felicity?

She gave herself a single, sharp nod. Only a trick of the light could leave her so breathless. That, and the exhilaration of nearly giving herself away.

"One more glance," Felicity whispered to herself around the thudding heart still stuck in her throat. "Prove to yourself that it was an illusion."

With a deep inhale, Felicity turned. She dared not poke so much as a toe out from the hedge this time. Instead, ducking this way and that, Felicity found enough of a window through the sculpted branches to peer through.

Felicity's heart drifted down to its rightful location. The man trotted up the front steps, his back to Felicity. She let out her breath in a long, slow exhale as he disappeared from view.

Alas, she had missed her chance to prove to herself that...that what? That Lady Swan's words were nothing more than a fanciful story?

Felicity clenched her fists at her sides. She had nothing to prove to anyone. They would all see in time and eventually surrender. Even that mysterious Lady Swan.

Felicity Reeve did not believe in romantic love. More importantly, Felicity Reeve did not lose.

CHAPTER THREE

T HAT BRIGHT LAUGH still lingered in the back of Atticus's mind even after two days of settling into his family's temporary home in Bainbridge and being introduced to a few prominent neighbors in the area. It provided a strangely welcome distraction from the merciless churning in his stomach as he leaned against the carriage window, his parents happily chatting between themselves on the seat across.

Shadows from overhanging trees dappled the cobbled street, transforming from one shape to another faster than Atticus could track. Had he imagined that laugh? He'd certainly imagined stranger things when lost in thought, either his own or, preferably, that of a brilliant and creative writer.

His heavy brows furrowed. No, there had been a very real quality about the sound, yet he had been unable to identify it in the moment. Its origin still eluded him.

The laugh, looping in his mind, ceased abruptly.

"You remember Lord and Lady Eldmar, do you not, Atticus?" Mama asked, pale-blue eyes aglow.

Atticus scrambled to correct his posture, bumping the brim of his hat into the window. Not that Mama or Papa cared much about his manners or nervous habits when they were alone. He sometimes disappeared so wholly into his mind or his books that it could be quite jarring when the real world demanded his attention.

"I do, I think," Atticus mumbled, grimacing as he searched for damage to his top hat. "They are the ones with a future duchess for a daughter, correct?"

"Indeed, and a son who married the daughter of a marquess!" Papa added, absentmindedly stroking his side-whiskers with one hand and nodding his approval.

Given the Wheadon family's lavish wealth, not much raised his parents' particular excitement, save for connections of the highest quality. They would be happy here in Bainbridge, where fine friendships were to be made around every corner. So it would be for Mama and Papa. For Atticus, the tale would be vastly different. It always was with him.

"I know I should not speak so hastily, and surely, now is not the right time to mention it, but Lady Eldmar did inform me when they called on us yesterday that they have two younger daughters, who came quite some time after the rest, as I understand it. Twins! Both are unmarried..."

Atticus stifled a groan and gave Mama a reluctantly encouraging smile.

The petite lady bounced in her seat, brown curls laced with gray swinging back and forth. "Oh, Atticus, surely one of them will catch your eye!"

"I promise to take that into consideration." Atticus chuckled with a timid attempt at a smile. The hand resting upon his knee clenched into a fist, palm slick.

The carriage slowed to a stop. Atticus's anxiety catapulted from the pit of his stomach to his throat, lodging behind his Adam's apple. Mama clapped her hands in excitement, peering up at the grand building through her window.

"See that you do, son," Papa added as he brushed away imaginary dust from his handsome coat. "Your younger sister was blessed to marry at twenty, and while we are overjoyed to have our first grandchild, Arabella's son will not inherit and carry on the Wheadon name or fortune. Only your sons can do that."

Atticus only had a moment to squeeze his eyes shut and

breathe. A footman opened the carriage door at the steps of Huxley Manor, the home of Viscount and Viscountess Eldmar and the location of a welcome luncheon hosted in the Wheadons' honor.

The last thing he needed when his nerves already quivered at the rapidly approaching afternoon full of strangers was to be reminded of the numerous great burdens on his shoulders—burdens he had never been sure he had the strength to carry. But with no brothers, each task fell solely to Atticus.

He was so discombobulated and the sun was so bright that he lost his footing on the way down from the carriage, nearly tripping again. His heart lurched in his chest...just like it had the day they had arrived, the day he had heard that distant laughter.

"Goodness, dear boy!" Mama gasped, grasping one of Atticus's elbows to steady him. She shot an amused glance to her husband. "Your father and I will leave the subject alone now." She chuckled. "We know how immersed you can become in your thoughts. But for this luncheon, try your best to stay present in the physical world. We must make an agreeable impression upon these people who are to be our society for who knows how long!"

Atticus forced a swallow, his throat painfully dry. "Of course I will do my best, Mama." He lowered his head respectfully, looped his mother's arm around his, and covered her hand where it rested in the crook of his arm.

The lady, nearly a head shorter than her oldest child, reached up and patted his cheek, thin with a prominent bone. "We know you will, darling Atticus. And one more thing: Do try to have fun."

At this, Atticus could only nod. Fun? Making shallow conversation with a handful of people he had only just met in the past two days and being trotted about for an entire village of strangers to gawk at? That was the very opposite of Atticus's idea of an enjoyable evening.

Yet it was the way of their world. It was a duty, even if some thrived in the execution of it, such as his parents. How Atticus had inherited none of their easy, pleasant, affable traits, he could not fathom. Even his dear sister, Arabella—now the eternally content Lady Hollington—though not as generally carefree as Mama and Papa, had been blessed with an outwardly affectionate character and the talent with which to wield it.

"Well, we should not keep our generous hosts waiting," Papa announced, taking Mama's free hand.

Atticus's chest constricted as they made their way up the front steps and followed the butler past stately columns into the Reeve family's beautiful home. Sweat beaded at his temples under dark, stubbornly disheveled hair. He could hardly take in the exquisite architecture and excellent artwork in the foyer and hallways for the thundering of his heart in his ears.

"Mr. and Mrs. Wheadon, and Mr. Atticus Wheadon," the broad-chested butler bellowed into the drawing room. A hush fell over the hum of light chatter. Every eye turned to Atticus and his family, the guests of honor, the fascinating novelties in an otherwise quiet and unvarying country life.

After offering the customary bow, Atticus struggled to force his head to remain upright. The weight on his neck and shoulders, the grip crushing his chest, made it nearly impossible to breathe, let alone maintain the proper, gentlemanly posture of unpretentious pride.

"Welcome, welcome," called Lady Eldmar, silken hands lifted upward as she floated across the drawing room toward the Wheadons, her smile glittering with hospitality. Tight ringlets, mostly gray with shadows of blonde, bounced in time with her measured steps.

The older adults attended to the standard warm greetings while Atticus lingered behind the barrier of his parents and nodded along at the appropriate times, only half-listening. From a trio of porcelain vases of varying heights in one corner to the potted fern in another to the nearly ceiling-to-floor portrait of some gallant, heroic colonel decorated in medals, Atticus's panicked eyes darted about the drawing room. Allowing them to land upon any other guests would be accidentally inviting a conversation.

"Right this way. I shall introduce you to all our dearest friends."

Atticus's mind spun with the sheer number of people in the large room as Lord and Lady Eldmar made introductions.

"This is Mr. Abbott and Lady Ainsworth."

"Ah, here are the Gardiners."

"And Mr. and Mrs. Harrowsmith, our newest couple!"

What felt like dozens of faces and names blurred together despite Atticus's best efforts to memorize them. The majority of his effort and energy always went to keeping his head bobbing up and down and his mouth mumbling superficial courtesies to appear as perfectly normal and friendly as possible.

Finally, after a torturous fifteen minutes of hearing the name of every resident and estate and how each was connected with the other, Atticus tasted his first breath of relief. Lady Eldmar concluded the introductions and captured Mama's arm, dragging her off toward the other mothers, while Lord Eldmar brought Papa to admire the painting of the colonel.

More than happy to be left on his own, Atticus sidled away to the unlit fireplace on the far wall, nursing the cup of tea the viscountess had given him, though he could not recall when. He wedged himself in the deep recess created by the ornate, marble fireplace and the built-in shelving beside it. Still visible to the crowd yet unobtrusive, uninviting.

Atticus had only managed to down a few sips of lukewarm tea when he felt that distressing tingle, the raising of bumps on his skin that could mean only one thing: eyes were upon him. Daring a glance of his own over the rim of his cup, Atticus quickly surveyed the room.

His stomach hollowed. Several young ladies, all of whom—including the younger Reeve twin—he had met just moments ago watched him with curiously raised brows from the opposite corner. Atticus adjusted the angle of his stance, providing them with only a side view.

Surely, they only paid particular attention to him because he was meant to be the focus of the day, as much as he abhorred the very notion. As patient and understanding as she was, Mama never allowed her son to neglect the social responsibility required of those blessed with their advantages. A necessary evil, one Atticus did not begrudge her for. The future head of a family such as theirs could not waste away as a recluse. It was entirely his fault that he was not suited to be a true member of Society.

"Ah, Lady Ainsworth."

The voice of the viscountess froze Atticus just as he'd summoned the courage to seek out a different hiding spot, one not in such direct view of the ladies. Lady Eldmar appeared on the other side of the fireplace, her back to Atticus. He pressed deeper into his nook, as uncomfortable as it was with his long, awkward limbs, just as Lady Eldmar beckoned to another guest.

"My lady?" asked Mr. Abbott's sister-in-law, the frequent chaperone to his daughter since Mrs. Abbott's passing, if Atticus recalled correctly. The younger woman, herself a widow, tilted her head to one side, long fingers absentmindedly tapping at her teacup.

Lady Eldmar shook her head, the emeralds in her hair twinkling. "No one has been able to locate Felicity," she hissed through gritted teeth, keeping her voice low. "I hoped she would have had the sense to be discovered by now. Instead, I was forced to introduce Mercy alone and embarrass myself by making excuses for Felicity's absence to our guests." The lines across her forehead and surrounding her mouth deepened. "You have the unhappy task of trailing after these girls all over the country. Have you any notion where the ingrate might be hiding?"

"On the contrary, Lady Eldmar," the dowager countess began with what sounded to Atticus like a strained chuckle. "I quite enjoy joining the young misses on their adventures. They are wonderful company."

For the first time that evening, Atticus felt the ghost of a smile on his lips, though his ears still burned red to hear the viscountess's unexpectedly severe criticism of her own child. At least Lady Ainsworth possessed the delicacy to check the other woman with a smile on her face and gentility in her voice.

"I swear," Lady Eldmar continued in a huff before allowing her friend to answer her query, "Felicity might be three-and-twenty, but I have been tempted to consider the idea of employing another governess to mind her for several more years. At the very least, I will be tightening the leading strings around her. Eventually, she will spend far too much energy being miserable to make much of a fuss."

A melancholy twinge struck Atticus square in the chest. His eyes dropped to the gleaming, hardwood floor, heat prickling his skin. He should not be hearing this. Surely, Miss Reeve's misery would only increase if she knew that a stranger had overheard her mother speak of her so unkindly. Atticus frowned at his shoes. He had not yet met the elder Reeve twin, yet Atticus could hardly fathom that any child deserved such insults and treatment from a parent.

"Perhaps try the garden," Lady Ainsworth offered after a long moment. "She often seeks fresh air when she feels overwhelmed."

Atticus's head snapped up. Yes, fresh air would be a delight.

"*Overwhelmed?*" Lady Eldmar barked under her breath. "What could possibly overwhelm the daughter of a viscount, of the most prominent family in Bainbridge?"

Resolve solidified inside Atticus. Miss Reeve had the right of it. Fresh air was just the thing, and surely, no one would miss him while they mingled prior to the meal. Everyone had already forgotten him, save for those young ladies.

As Lady Ainsworth led the exasperated viscountess to a pair of nearby chairs, Atticus made his escape, skirting the edge of the room and muttering excuses over his shoulder. Unsurprisingly, no one made any fuss over his temporary departure, thoroughly engaged in their own conversations.

The moment he slipped through the drawing room doors, blessed air filled Atticus's lungs. His chest, broad despite his lean frame, expanded with the sweet aroma of solitude—that, and the evenly spaced display tables bearing bowls of citrus fruits lining the hallway.

"May I assist you, sir? Are you unwell?"

Atticus jolted at the quiet voice's sudden intrusion, his eyes flying open. A perplexed maid, arms brimming with linens, watched Atticus from a respectful distance and curtseyed when their gazes met.

"P-Perfectly well, thank you. Might you point me in the direction of the gardens? If it is no trouble, of course."

Following the maid's instructions, Atticus wound his way through Lord and Lady Eldmar's grand home until he finally emerged into the sunlight and summer breeze of the back terrace. He took the steps down onto the lawn two at a time, long legs carrying him quickly down the gravel path to the promise of private greenery in the distance.

With every step, with every songbird's melody and every wispy cloud drifting across the blue sky, Atticus's spirits lifted. Not by any great degree, yet he welcomed even minuscule improvements in the distress running rampant in his mind by whatever means he could achieve them.

Seeking comfort in the outdoors had never been Atticus's preferred method. It was still the vastly superior choice to remaining in the drawing room or attempting to find familiarity in another's library. Though Setherwell did indeed boast an expansive library, it did not yet possess the creature comforts of Atticus's library at home, a fact he had already begun to remedy.

For once, all thoughts of books disappeared from Atticus's mind as he came upon the gardens, enclosed by neat hedges with paths that led toward a pavilion in the center. Beyond the structure stretched rows upon rows of bushes in full bloom, some bearing flowers completely foreign to Atticus's eye. The gardens of Huxley Manor were beautiful. Atticus sighed, a heavenly, floral scent drifting toward him on the wind, and offered a silent prayer of thanks for the opportunity to appreciate this place in solitude and peace.

Walking slowly down a row of rosebushes, grateful for the calm, steady pace of his own heartbeat and the easy flow of his breath, Atticus allowed his fingertips to trail across soft petals. Some were red, some white, others the palest blush while still more displayed vibrant shades of orange and yellow. Had he ever seen roses of such magnificent variety?

He had certainly not seen any rogue young ladies.

"So, you have finally found your footing."

Atticus nearly jumped out of his skin. He clutched his chest and doubled over as if he had just seen a dreadful apparition.

There was nothing dreadful about the chestnut-brown eyes staring back at him from around the next rosebush, the faint lines at the corners betraying their owner's mirth.

Curls bouncing, the presumed Miss Reeve hurried out from behind the bush, her pale-pink dress glittering and plump lips fighting a battle between an amused smile and a concerned frown. Gloved hands shot out and grasped Atticus's arm, steadying him.

"Heavens! Is it too soon for me to beg your forgiveness for causing your heart to stop?"

The lady laughed. Atticus's heart indeed stopped.

"It is you," he whispered.

Somewhere in the back of his mind, Atticus's propriety shouted that this strange, young woman was still touching him, still holding on to him. The sheer awe at finding himself standing before the answer he had hardly been aware of seeking overwhelmed all other senses.

"It is I," she answered, each syllable lifted by an airy giggle. Her eyes dropped to the insignificant stretch of gravel path separating his polished boots from the tips of her satin slippers, peeking out from under an embroidered hem. Her hands slipped back to her sides as well.

"I suppose now is as good a time as any," she continued, "to beg your forgiveness for my previous transgression of covertly observing your arrival. My curiosity got the better of me, you see. I am Miss Felicity Reeve."

Miss Reeve's gaze flew back up to meet Atticus's. His eyes widened at the healthy dose of pride he saw there. Such fearlessness was utterly foreign to him. He could not begin to imagine what a wonder this lady must have been to possess the skill of conveying confidence even within her remorse.

Atticus's heart ceased its erratic hammering and settled into a dizzying buzz.

Yet it did not feel quite the same as when his incessant fears of the future overtook him or when he drowned in an ocean of conversation. He did not feel on the verge of imploding. Rather the opposite, in fact. If his heart fluttered any faster, he might drift off into the endless summer sky. What an odd sensation, and at such a peculiar time!

"Truly, I am sor—"

"No, please," Atticus said in a rush, shaking his head. "One apology was unnecessary already. You have done nothing that warrants it. In fact, I welcome any and all heart stopping and covert observing you wish to do."

As soon as the words stumbled from his lips, Atticus grimaced inwardly. Why did he always say such strange things when faced with even the simplest pressure?

Miss Reeve chuckled. "Are you not supposed to be inside for the luncheon, Mr....?"

"Atticus Wheadon." He quickly offered a stiff bow. "Now I must beg your forgiveness, Miss Reeve, for the terribly unfortunate nature of our first introduction."

The young lady shrugged. "I found it more invigorating than unfortunate."

Atticus's eyes widened. A shrug before a stranger! Miss Reeve truly was a bold woman. Nor had anyone ever described Atticus or anything to do with him as "invigorating."

When he lapsed into silence once more, a regrettable habit that often resulted in some embarrassment for him, Miss Reeve lifted a dark brow. "You are here for the luncheon, are you not?" "Yes, yes, indeed." Atticus nodded, thankful for Miss Reeve's polite prompt. "It is just that I overheard her—well, this is a bit more..." Biting the inside of his cheek, Atticus slipped a finger under his collar and tugged, suddenly aware of just how bright and full the sun shone up above.

Miss Reeve's open, spirited countenance transformed in less than the blink of an eye. Her narrow shoulders drooped, a scowl twisting delicate features into sharp, cold anger. Even the honey-blonde curls framing her face seemed to freeze.

"The viscountess."

Atticus's mouth pressed into a hard line. He lowered his gaze. Clearly, the feelings of animosity and resentment flowed passionately in both directions between Lady Eldmar and Miss Reeve.

"Your mother, yes. I thought someone ought to inform you that she is searching for you and she is...not pleased."

Miss Reeve heaved an exasperated sigh and crossed her arms, still unconcerned with ladylike decorum. Once assured that she remained distracted enough with her own internal deliberations, Atticus allowed himself to admire the lady.

He had spent his entire life being as unobtrusive as possible to avoid attracting attention. Here Miss Reeve stood, his perfect opposite, someone so comfortable in herself that she did not hide any part, even when making the all-important first impression.

"I suppose I have delayed long enough if even the guest of honor seeks to drag me back," she grumbled after a long moment.

Atticus's eyes widened. "No, Miss Reeve, not at all." He held up both hands, palms forward, pleading with the lady. "I would never dare seek to drag you anywhere. I doubt you would go, in any case. I only sought to inform."

"You doubt it, do you?" Miss Reeve laughed quietly, her icy

expression thawing.

Before the panic of unintentionally causing offense could rise in Atticus again, she continued. "Well, there is nothing for it but to meet our fates up there."

Remembering his manners, Atticus offered his arm to the lady. Warmth simmered inside him at the feeling of her touch on his person once more. It was familiar and full of life, two things he could not possibly claim to know about Miss Reeve after speaking for a few minutes.

Atticus did his best to ignore the feeling as they slowly made their way back through the gardens, past the pavilion and trimmed hedges, and into the house. Miss Reeve offered no conversation, her gaze hard and withdrawn, eyes narrowed as they stared straight ahead.

For some reason, despite Atticus's eternal preference for silence and solitude, the anger and frustration wafting off the woman beside him stirred his heart. Without fully realizing what he was doing, Atticus stopped halfway up the stairs.

"Why do you not wish to participate in the luncheon?"

Miss Reeve, a foot already raised, paused on the step above Atticus. Her sour expression gave way to confusion. Embarrassment scorched every inch of Atticus's skin. He quickly lowered his eyes, now nearly level with Miss Reeve's.

"F-Forgive me for such an impertinent question," he stammered. "We are hardly more than strangers. I have no right—"

That laugh again. It was not as light, carefree this time. Bitterness underscored the sound. Atticus dared to look up. Miss Reeve offered a forlorn smile that somehow resembled more of a frown.

"I was not expecting a stranger to care." With a sharp exhale, the lady turned her face away and jutted her chin into the air. "Most of the strangers I meet are only concerned with the bland review of me Lady Eldmar provides, accomplishments and dowries and all that. But once they catch a glimpse of something that cannot be abridged in a few superficial sentences... Of course, you need not know any of this."

Words failed Atticus. He had not been expecting such truth, nor could he fathom what it must be like to live with such feelings—to so clearly desire love and acceptance, only to be met with criticism and rejection. Despite meeting Lord and Lady Eldmar only yesterday and meeting their youngest children not fifteen minutes prior, Atticus felt he had come to know enough of their familial relationships—not entirely willingly—to be confident in his assumption.

"A shame, indeed," was all he could manage to whisper, nodding his head in understanding.

Though Atticus had always known men and women were born to carry different pressures, he had never truly heard any member of the opposite sex share Miss Reeve's unflattering opinions on the obligations with which she was raised. His sister's only complaint had been that she could not dance more than two sets with the dashing Baron Hollington until they married. As much as Atticus dreaded the weight of his future, to hear Miss Reeve touch upon her struggles afforded him a greater appreciation for his fate.

Miss Reeve's soft cheekbones colored a subtle, lovely pink as she turned on her heel and continued up the stairs. Atticus waited for her to ascend a few steps before following.

He did not know how he knew that Miss Reeve required some distance to collect herself. Perhaps, because he was so familiar with the sensation himself, he could now identify it in others. Yet Atticus did not understand why she looked over her shoulder at him every few seconds, as if reassuring herself that he was there. Nor did he understand why he should have developed such an impression.

Before Atticus could untangle it all, they reached the landing. The sound of muffled conversation drifted down the hall. Inviting to most, perilous to Atticus.

"I fear we are both quite trapped now." Miss Reeve groaned. She glanced at Atticus from the corner of her eye. "Shall we?"

"We shall," Atticus answered, offering his arm once more.

Side by side, they marched toward the drawing room and whatever agony awaited them.

"You wait here. Just a few minutes should do," Miss Reeve announced as they paused before the doors. She pulled away and turned to face Atticus, wearing a half-smile. "And when my poor, harried mother introduces us, do feel free to feign your surprise at my beauty."

Atticus swallowed. "O-Of course."

Her smile widened. "I am only joking. Though I suppose you must have already met Mercy, in which case my countenance would hardly surprise you. Now, wish me luck."

"Best of luck, Miss Reeve," Atticus mumbled as the young lady faced the doors, stiffened her shoulders, and lifted her chin.

She slipped into the drawing room, leaving Atticus to wonder how the visage of one identical twin could already fade to the back of his mind while the other had commanded all his attention from the moment their eyes had met.

CHAPTER FOUR

"**Y**OU ARE BREATHTAKING, Felicity!" Clara squealed as quietly as possible, guests filtering around the group of young ladies gathered in the foyer of Setherwell Court.

Ellen, hands clasped under her chin as if in prayer, nodded her enthusiastic agreement. She glowed in her lilac gown under the chandelier's generous light, the angelic beauty to her younger sister's vibrant handsomeness.

All of Felicity's friends looked wonderful in their finest evening gowns for the Wheadon family's first ball. Yet she was the one standing in the middle of their circle, neck long and head held high—no easy feat, considering the heaps of jewels Lady Eldmar had insisted on weaving into her hair.

"The viscountess remained true to her word," Isabel said, green eyes tracing the delicate, golden embroidery over the cream silk of Felicity's newest dress. "She truly is sparing no expense for your appearance now."

"Oh, hush, all of you." Felicity swatted a hand, not bothering to disguise her proud smile. "Has no one a kind word to spare for my sister? Her gown is as new and beautiful as mine, is it not?"

She waved a hand to her left, where Mercy had taken up a spot next to Lydia in Felicity's circle of admirers. Despite being quite identical—and thus able to assume that any compliment to one's appearance applied equally to the other—neither twin appreciated being treated as one merely to save someone else the effort of politeness. Felicity knew that not to be the case here among their lifelong friends, but she did not wish to acknowledge their true intent in singling her out for praise she could not help absorbing.

"We did pay dear Mercy our compliments when we arrived," Lydia said, her peacock-blue gown a lovely contrast to the lighter shade of her observant eyes. "Or did you pay them no mind because they were not directed at you?" she added with a surprisingly teasing smile. Being married to Sebastian had already done wonders to ease the rigidity bred into Lydia by her austere mother.

"Come along now, all of you!" called kind Mr. Abbott from the foot of the wide staircase in the center of the foyer, surrounded by their waiting families.

Taking one last moment to adjust each other's necklaces and pinch each other's already rouged cheeks, the ladies followed the rest of their group up to the ballroom, whispering words of encouragement and tenderhearted hopes. All save for Felicity. She had no need for encouragement and she certainly harbored no tenderhearted hopes.

"You look so beautiful, I am sure Mr. Atticus Wheadon will end the night in love with you. Lady Swan shall be correct once more!" Clara whispered to Felicity, leaning in close as the ballroom doors opened before them. A cascade of music and laughter spilled out.

Felicity lifted her nose in the air and glanced at her friends from the corner of her eye. "On the contrary, Clara. In fact, all of you should heed my words. I am going to prove to you all that Mr. Atticus Wheadon and I would be the most ill-suited match to ever appear before an altar. He is so very...strained and...humble."

She suppressed the giggle that bubbled to her lips at the memory of his strangely charming awkwardness, molding it into a grin that spread from ear to ear as the other ladies shook their heads at Felicity's stubbornness. Their doubt only inspired greater confidence in herself. No matter how different Mr. Wheadon might seem from most gentlemen, she would not be a pawn in this inane, little ploy by some writer hiding behind anonymity with nothing else to occupy her time. Lady Swan's scheme to throw together such opposites was no match for Felicity's competitive nature.

Until she turned at precisely the wrong moment. The first person Felicity's eyes landed upon was none other than Mr. Atticus Wheadon himself. He stared back from across the ballroom wearing that same wide-eyed expression as he had when she had nearly startled the life out of him.

Her heart...fluttered. No, it was a spasm. Surely, that was it. A thrill of anticipation for a lively ball with all her favorite country neighbors.

It could have nothing to do with Mr. Wheadon. It could have nothing to do with the fact that the very same sensation had seized her for the first time in her life that day in the gardens, nearly a week ago now. Not that Felicity had been counting.

She had nearly forgotten that strange feeling. She had been trying to forget it.

"Ah, there is the younger Mr. Wheadon." Lydia subtly pointed to the corner, as far from the dance floor as possible. "And it appears he has already noticed you, Felicity."

Felicity tore her eyes away and glared at her friends, their parents busy with greeting the host and hostess as well as the other guests nearest the doors. "He could be looking at Mercy for all we know. No one can tell one from another at this distance."

"He is not looking at me, sister," Mercy quietly rebutted. She lifted one shoulder in an apologetic shrug when Felicity rounded on her.

Of course Mercy knew how frustrating it was for her twin to endure the others' good-natured speculation and coaxing in conjunction with Lady Eldmar's efforts. She did what she could to remain on Felicity's side, yet Felicity knew she would not lie if pressed.

"He will not remove his eyes from you!" Clara cried, nearly bouncing on her toes. At least the pearls in her light-red hair had been fixed quite firmly in place.

"'Dearest Miss Reeve, I pray my gaze is communicating my ardent love to you across this vast distance that wickedly separates us.'" Isabel sighed, pitching her voice a touch lower in a poor attempt to mimic the man.

"I have already been swept off my feet, Mr. Wheadon!" Clara replied as she whipped her fan open and swished it before her face.

Taking advantage of the cacophony in the ballroom, Felicity let out a groan. She supposed the ladies had earned the right to turn her own dramatics and love for jests against her every now and again. As their families dispersed throughout the massive ballroom, ornately decorated in shimmering golds and fresh blooms, the group of friends turned its attention to the nearest sideboard, filling plates with sharp cheeses and succulent fruits.

"Do you still believe Lady Swan is mistaken after seeing the way Mr. Wheadon is watching you?" prodded Lydia.

Felicity bit down hard on the delicious strawberry she had been so looking forward to enjoying. A familiar pressure settled on the small of Felicity's back, Mercy appearing at her side.

"It matters not if Lady Swan is mistaken," Mercy replied as her twin chewed. "Felicity does not desire any shackles, no matter how well-fitting."

Swallowing, Felicity nodded along. Just as Lydia opened her mouth to politely counter, Lady Swan's praises no doubt on the tip of her tongue, Felicity's eyes betrayed her once more.

How, in this expansive room brimming with all of Bainbridge, did they always land on *him*?

The crowd lingering nearest the enthusiastic musicians broke apart, providing Felicity a clearer view of the younger Mr. Wheadon's slow approach. Mr. and Mrs. Wheadon had apparently captured their son in the corner and were now shooing him along to the area's most promising potential brides.

Felicity straightened her shoulders. She had faced every challenge in life squarely. This one would be no different...even if the man's wringing hands and round eyes were a little endearing. Only a little.

"Mr. Wheadon! Please do join us," called Clara, their friendliest and most romantically inclined member, before Felicity could protest.

The gentleman's only reply was a tight smile.

"Please offer our compliments to your parents on a beautiful evening," Ellen added, her voice barely audible over the music and chatter.

"I-I certainly will. Thank you, Miss Gardiner."

He lowered his head respectfully, though Felicity could not help noticing the fevered twitching of his fingers at his sides. How could he be nervous around Ellen, the sweetest soul to have ever graced this Earth?

With an unreadable expression that did not sit well with Felicity, Isabel stepped forward. "Have you enjoyed many dances thus far?"

Felicity's mouth went dry at Isabel's obvious glance and pleased air. She looked as though she were about to prove that Mr. Wheadon had been impatiently awaiting Felicity's arrival, forsaking all others. Somehow, Lady Swan had convinced even practical and analytical Isabel that this complete stranger had already fallen in love with Felicity.

Mr. Wheadon chuckled, his gaze darting over each of the ladies' faces, seemingly unsure where to look or how long to linger. "I must confess I am far too ungainly to make a respectable dancer. But I very much enjoy observing the skills of others."

"Then you *must* dance with our Felicity!" Clara clapped, silk gloves muffling the sound. "She is the finest dancer of us all and easily makes up for any deficiencies in her partner."

The air disappeared from their little assembly. Lydia's mouth nearly fell open at Clara's accidental insult while Mercy began sputtering an explanation.

Felicity did not hear it. Neither did Mr. Wheadon, it seemed. His gaze held hers, steady. His entire being was still.

"I have not had the pleasure of knowing Miss Reeve long, but I sensed the very same."

Felicity's eyes widened, a breath catching in her throat. Why would he say such a thing when he hardly knew her? When she had been clear not to display any of the genteel qualities men sought in wives? Why did he insist on surprising her? *She* was the one who did the surprising.

"Miss Reeve—"

He reached toward her. Fear seized Felicity's heart. This should not be happening. She jerked back, his fingertips just barely brushing the bare skin of her arm above her long evening gloves.

Even that whisper of a touch singed. She took another half-step back, remembering too late the looming, white, stone column behind her bearing a tall vase of plump, yellow blooms.

The back of her head thumped solidly against the column's rounded corner. Felicity's entire world swam for one strange, glorious, aching moment. Her piles of curls and gemstones had done nothing to shield the blow.

"Miss Reeve!"

That voice, usually so timorous, called unwaveringly to her as if from a great distance, yet it rang in her ears at the same time, bouncing around her mind, separate from her yet part of her at the same time. Large, expressive, cornflower-blue eyes rushed toward her, full of concern.

For a fleeting, foolish moment, a vision flashed through Felicity's blurry thoughts, as bright and clear as day. Falling asleep in a bed of cornflowers in late-afternoon sunlight. Would such a thing truly be so terrible?

One firm hand shot out with urgency and grasped Felicity's arm while the other reached behind, steadying the precarious vase.

Felicity's senses rushed back in an instant. She immediately became aware of Mr. Wheadon's closeness, his outstretched arm creating a protective circle around her as he held the vase in place, drawing her against his chest.

She also became aware of the dull throbbing in her head, already fading with every passing moment. And the feeling of every gaze in the room on her, including those of her distressed friends and her quietly vexed mother.

Gathering her wits as best she could, Felicity forced herself to look up at Mr. Wheadon, the man who had just saved her from making an even greater fool of herself in the middle of a teeming ballroom. Yet had he not been the cause of Felicity's misstep in the first place?

"Thank you," she whispered.

That was all she could muster. He deserved that much, after all. Even if he did supposedly pose a threat to Felicity's plans for her future, at least according to Lady Swan. Even if he did make Felicity's heart do strange things.

"Are you injured?" Mr. Wheadon demanded. His earnest gaze searched her face for an answer, perhaps looking for a wince or the first sign of drooping eyelids.

Felicity carefully shook her head. The longer she stared at Mr. Wheadon like this, herself now the wide-eyed, tongue-tied one, the less she noticed any discomfort or anomalies resulting from her clumsy encounter.

"It seems we are destined to meet under strange circumstances," he said with a quiet laugh.

Felicity laughed, too. "You hardly know the half of it."

Mr. Wheadon's thick brows furrowed, a crease appearing between them, in that same endearingly perplexed expression. "What do you—"

"Sister! Shall we send for a physician?"

Felicity felt Mercy's presence by her side before she saw her. Turning, she found her friends cloistering behind Mercy, wanting to be near without crowding.

As if suddenly aware of the very public view of this intimate posture, Mr. Wheadon quickly released Felicity. He took a respectful step back, worrying at the cuff of his coat sleeve.

Felicity immediately missed the stability of his presence, both physical and emotional. Despite his awkwardness, the gentleman possessed a calming, steadying spirit that had been evident from their first meeting. Her knees wobbled.

Without a word passed between them, the Bainbridge ladies encircled Felicity. Mercy slipped an arm around her twin's waist and Ellen did the same on the other side. The gathering dispersed and merriment resumed as Lydia led them toward a quieter corner, fanning Felicity's flushed face all the while.

She had not yet managed to answer a single one of her friends' overlapping questions when, without warning, Lady Eldmar appeared behind their protective wall.

"Daughter." The viscountess's voice cut through the babble, clear and steely.

"Mother." Felicity rose from the chair Isabel had procured. Straightening her spine, she pushed past her friends.

Felicity had never allowed the older woman to see any weakness or fear. She certainly did not intend to start now.

"My poor, dear daughter, please tell me you are unharmed," Lady Eldmar continued, the elegant lines of her figure softening into a mask of concern as she cupped Felicity's face in both hands.

Only Felicity and Mercy could see the anger brimming in her dark eyes.

She did not wait for an answer before turning her attention to the gentleman lingering a respectful distance away, back pressed to the wall, and waving. The younger Mr. Wheadon answered the viscountess's summons, though he appeared to be doing his best to avoid looking anyone in the eye for more than two seconds.

"Thank you, sir, for bravely coming to my daughter's aid." Lady Eldmar sighed as she dabbed at imaginary tears with a handkerchief. "I cannot begin to express how sorry I am that she has imposed upon you, and I shall be sure to repeat the sentiments to your parents as soon as I have finished tending to my precious Felicity."

"T-Truly, my lady, it is never any trouble—"

Tucking her handkerchief away and snapping her reticule shut, Lady Eldmar excused herself and Felicity and began the long march toward the ballroom doors, Mercy following in their wake. To her credit, the viscountess accepted each sympathetic look and concerned inquiry with remarkable grace. One would never know that she disdained the very same child she doted upon in public.

Felicity's head remained lowered as she followed her mother out into the hallway, patrolled by harried footmen. The moment the doors closed behind them, she lifted it. The subtle change in position sent a pulsing ache to the back of her head. It would remain sore for some days, no doubt, a vexing reminder of a night Felicity longed to forget yet knew she would repeat in her mind later—certain parts of it, at least.

Lady Eldmar spun to face Felicity. Every ounce of parental concern she had shown in the ballroom amongst their friends, neighbors, and acquaintances had evaporated. The woman's fists clenched at her sides. Felicity braced herself.

"I swear, you have been determined to send me to an early grave from the very moment of your birth!" the viscountess screeched. From the corner of her eye, Felicity saw Mercy flinch.

"After all I endured for you, *this* is how you repay me? By humiliating me with your foolishness?" she continued, jabbing an accusatory finger at Felicity from across the hallway. Her growing fury prevented her from coming any nearer.

"Your exemplary education and training in deportment have proven to be an utter waste." The viscountess threw her hands into the air and shook her head before rounding on the elder twin once more. "Are you truly determined to remain unmarried? Because you have surely sealed that fate tonight. No man in that room, nor anyone to whom those men might gossip, will accept you after that blundering display."

Fire seared Felicity's throat. She scoffed through the pain. "How nice of you to finally realize it, Mother. Yes, I am indeed determined to remain unwed. I shall live with Mercy when she inevitably marries, or with one of my friends as a companion. As I have said time and time again. Not that you have ever been near enough to hear it." Felicity waved a hand toward the ballroom. "If this is what it takes to finally impress that message upon you, then so be it."

Lady Eldmar gasped, pale skin taut, ashy curls quivering. "How dare you, you wretched—"

"Mother, please!" Mercy cried, rushing into the middle of the hallway between her mother and sister, slippers muffled by the plush rug. "Please return to the ball. Return to your friends and refreshments. I shall remain here with Felicity until she is recovered."

At this, the younger twin shot a warning glance over her shoulder at the elder. Felicity clenched her teeth and gave a single grudging nod of agreement, ignoring the flames of fury coursing in her veins.

"Very well," Lady Eldmar barked. Her chest, draped in glittering diamonds, heaved up and down. "I can no longer stand to look upon you," she spat as she stormed past Felicity and Mercy. The ripple of air that accompanied her stung with chill.

Alone but for servants going about their missions, the twins groaned in unison. "Well, that was terrible." Mercy rubbed at her temples while Felicity clenched and unclenched her fingers at her sides, collecting themselves.

After a moment, Mercy returned her attention to her older sister, taking one fist and easing it open enough to slip her hand in.

"The viscountess did not ask if you were well, not truly," she said quietly. "Are you well, Felicity? Injuries to the head are not to be trifled with. Even minor injuries can be deceptive—"

Felicity interrupted her. "I am perfectly well, Mercy, I promise." Her lips, pressed into a hard line, relaxed into a grateful smile. She adjusted her hand to thread her fingers through her twin's.

Mercy fell silent. Her observant eyes—so different from the intensity of Felicity's—searched for any trace of a lie. "But it did look like quite a hearty thump," she pressed.

"It was more shocking than harmful, I rather think," Felicity insisted with a chuckle. "Though I imagine I will be sleeping on my side for a few nights until this dreadful growth recedes."

"Growth?!"

Felicity laughed, relishing the warmth and weightlessness of the feeling. She desperately needed some cheer after all that nonsense.

"I jest, my darling Mercy. There is no growth." She reached up and forced a finger through the mess of intricate ringlets at the back of her head and hissed. "Only a bruise, thank goodness. And all my faculties appear as sound as ever—which is not necessarily the most comforting endorsement, now that I think of it."

Glowering, Mercy dropped Felicity's hand and thrust her nose up. "Then I suppose you will not mind if I comment on how heroically Mr. Wheadon behaved."

In the blink of an eye, Felicity's good humor vanished. She knit her brows low over her nose and frowned, mirroring Mercy's expression.

Even her own twin, the other half of her mind, had taken up Lady Swan's cause. Felicity crossed her arms and shook her head.

"Do you truly think I should have anything to do with someone so timid and apprehensive? You recall what he was like during the luncheon. He conversed with no one—not even me, after the garden—and looked more inclined to sink through the floor than participate in a simple card game. We cannot possibly share any common interests or inclinations." She groaned.

Yet as the words left her lips, her heart twinged. Something was wrong. She was not being entirely fair to his character. But what did his character matter when Felicity had always known what she wanted? What could be more liberating than living the remainder of her days by her twin's side, or under the roof of one of her dearest friends, with no one to command or criticize her?

To Felicity's increasing frustration, Mercy averted her gaze and began twiddling her thumbs. "If Lady Swan clearly believes there is potential..."

Felicity's mouth ripped open to demand to know when, exactly, Mercy had betrayed her. Behind them, the ballroom doors burst wide, illuminating the sisters in the light of innumerable candles. The one who rushed out took no notice of them.

Mr. Atticus Wheadon's long legs carried him down the hallway faster than Felicity would have guessed possible. His head remained bowed all the while, eyes on the floor.

"What do you think might have caused that?" Mercy whispered as the gentleman's broad-shouldered outline disappeared into the shadows.

"I have not the faintest idea," Felicity lied.

Perhaps it was not a lie. Perhaps Felicity only *thought* she knew what had disturbed Mr. Wheadon. The almost-imperceptible voice in the back of her mind told her that she was not wrong, though she truly had no reason to be right.

She *did* know precisely what bothered him. But she had noticed, or rather sensed, his nervous habits from the moment they'd met. Tonight, the anxiety and overwhelming discomfort had been writ large on his face. He must have reached his threshold.

Without paying any mind to what she did, Felicity took a step.

CHAPTER FIVE

O NLY WHEN MERCY grasped Felicity's wrist with both hands and yanked her back did she realize she had been going into the darkness…after Mr. Atticus Wheadon.

"What in the heavens, pray tell, has possessed you?" Mercy gasped in an urgent whisper. "You cannot follow after a strange man down a dark hall to who knows where! You may have made a point of your disregard for the *ton*'s edicts to all who know you, yet even those who are familiar with your shocking behavior will never allow you to recover from *that*."

"He is not strange…" Felicity said under her breath, again without thinking, without giving herself a chance to reconsider. "Well, he *is* a bit strange, but in a good way."

Mercy frowned. "Is there such a thing as a good way to be strange?"

For reasons beyond Felicity's present understanding, she bristled at her twin's words. "I wish to inquire after his health. He did just come to my aid, after all. You are welcome to join if you wish to be useful and keep watch for me."

She did not wait for an answer. Turning on her heel, Felicity marched deeper down the hallway. Mercy's familiar footsteps swished softly against the rug, following quickly.

No tall, angular figure appeared before her, no matter how far Felicity walked down that long path, the sounds of a lively evening fading behind her. Her eyes had just fixed upon a footman up ahead whom she prayed had seen where his young master had gone when they came upon a well-lit staircase. Felicity could just make out the disheveled, mahogany-brown head bobbing down the stairs through the carved wood banister.

Felicity ignored her sister's squirm of discomfort and hastened her steps so as not to lose sight of Mr. Wheadon again. Mercy still followed, always loyal to Felicity's wildest fancies. On the floor below, Mr. Wheadon disappeared behind a heavy, oak door, leaving it open just enough for Felicity to spy the library beyond.

An unexpected smile tugged at her lips as she slowed to a furtive tiptoe. She was not surprised that his refuge was the library. Why did she feel as though she understood this man when nothing could be further from the truth?

Without hesitation, Felicity stepped one foot over the threshold.

Mercy once again grabbed hold of her sister's wrist. "Felicity, you cannot truly mean to enter that room...to be alone with him! This is not like before, when you told me he found you in the garden. That was in broad daylight, in full view of any number of servants who might validate your claims of innocence if anyone asked—though even that situation was already quite a leap from propriety. But this... I shall enter with you, at least."

Felicity could only stare into the shadows of the library, flickering in the light of a distant fireplace.

A powerful force for which she had no name, because she had never felt such a thing in her three-and-twenty years, called to her heart. It beat hard and insistent in reply, longing to follow...to see if Lady Swan was correct after all.

"Leave the door fully open. You wait outside," she instructed, her own voice muffled against the drumming in her chest.

"Felicity."

The sharpness in Mercy's voice forced Felicity back to cold reality.

"You know this would lead to my ruination as well as your

own."

Felicity could only meet her twin's perfectly just and sensible sharpness with the earnest emotion in her eyes. She knew her oldest and dearest friend would feel it.

"I need to see if he is well."

Mercy's frown eased into a reluctant pout. She nodded and took up her post at the doorway.

To Felicity's relief, the smoldering fire revealed that Mr. Wheadon had not already disappeared into the impressively labyrinthine shelves of Setherwell's library. In fact, he had not gone very far at all.

The gentleman braced one hand against a shelf along the left wall, his shoulders rounded and head lowered. Even in this dim light, Felicity could see the tremor of labored breathing.

A fear she had not been aware of until it had come to fruition seized her chest. He truly was not well at all.

Hoping not to startle the poor man, Felicity slipped closer with lighter footwork than had ever graced any ballroom. She cleared the nervous lump in her throat.

He spun around, panic ablaze in his eyes.

They squeezed shut when the gentleman saw Felicity. His breathing slowed.

"Miss Reeve, are you in need of assist—Good heavens, you should not be in here."

His caring first instinct was not lost on Felicity. Warmth flooded her from the center of her chest outward. She did her best to brush that aside. Now was not the time to determine what that might signify.

"Do not fret over where I should or should not be, Mr. Wheadon. I can manage myself," Felicity replied in a forced factual tone.

Mr. Wheadon took a step closer, his hand sliding off the shelf, long fingers trailing over leather spines.

Strange how Felicity's senses seemed to flee at the precise moments she needed them most. Once more without thinking, she found herself matching his movement, bringing them nearly toe to toe.

"I certainly have no doubt of that," he said, worrying at the sleeves of his coat, "but I am afraid you are putting yourself at grave risk in the eyes of Society at this very moment. I am certainly not worth the repercussions you would suffer should we be found."

Felicity wrinkled her nose. "I know the rules well enough. What I do not know and what I must know immediately is if you are unwell."

The raised brows and slightly ajar mouth of his surprised expression were so endearing that Felicity failed to suppress her blush. She offered a silent plea to the heavens that the dimness of the library would conceal what she could not. How could a grown man look so...darling?

"Why?" Mr. Wheadon asked, so quietly, Felicity would not have heard if she had not been so close. They were, indeed, very, very close.

In an effort to distract herself from the fact, Felicity huffed and crossed her arms. She had already broken enough rules in this man's presence that another transgression seemed negligible. "I noticed you seemed unwell earlier and wanted to be sure you were being tended to. I am merely returning your helpful deed."

The gentleman gave a small smile and lowered his head respectfully. "I am quite well now, thanks to you, Miss Reeve. I am ever grateful for your kind attention."

In the silence that followed, the only thing Felicity heard was the fluttering of her own heart. What on Earth was happening to her?

Before Felicity could lose herself down that convoluted path of thought that would yield no satisfying answers, Mr. Wheadon's face transformed before her eyes.

From quiet contentment to pure horror.

The carefree wings of the butterflies in Felicity's stomach crumpled. Her very blood frozen, Felicity turned.

The viscountess's shadow filled the doorway of the library. Mercy hovered behind her with head bowed, hands twisting her ivory skirts.

Felicity's insides twisted into sickening shapes.

"M-My lady, please allow me to explain—"

"Mother, it is not what you think—"

"Silence."

Felicity snapped her mouth shut immediately, a true rarity. Judging by the way Mr. Wheadon's lips muttered silently, Felicity guessed that he was praying for a miracle to deliver them from this dreadful dream. At least, it certainly was a dreadful dream for Felicity.

Lady Eldmar only came a few more steps into the library. Surely, even with the dying flames in the fireplace, she could see how close her daughter stood to an unmarried man, completely unchaperoned in a dark room.

"Already sneaking away for privacy? Well, if you are that smitten with each other, there is only one thing for it."

A painful lump launched itself into Felicity's throat. "No, Mother," she croaked, her mind spinning too fast to formulate a coherent sentence. "We do not feel—I do not feel—I only meant—"

"That hardly matters now, does it?" Lady Eldmar clapped her hands together. "I must say, I did not think this would be the way I finally got you down the aisle. Not ideal, to be sure, but in a few years' time, no one will remember your *hasty courtship*, as we shall all exclusively refer to it from this moment forth."

The spinning stopped. Felicity's mind went blank as her mother's words rang in her ears. The floor beneath her feet became more like sand than solid wood.

"My lady, I know you have no reason to trust my word, stranger to you that I am, but I can assure you that nothing untoward occurred or would have occurred. Miss Reeve only sought to look after me when she noticed I was in distress, but as the moment had passed, we were just preparing to return."

Felicity was only vaguely aware of the surprising strength in Mr. Wheadon's voice, of the comforting pressure of his arm against hers. They stood side by side, facing the ends of both their lives as they knew them.

"That is all lovely, but I am afraid none of that matters, either. Or are you informing me that you refuse to take responsibility for my daughter's honor?"

Even in the dying firelight, Felicity could see the calculating tilt of her mother's head. No, the woman had hammered the nails into the coffin of Felicity's freedom the moment she'd seen them alone. Felicity was certain she knew nothing untoward had happened and could allow this to be swept away, yet still, she did not care. There would be no amount of begging equal enough to Lady Eldmar's pleasure in ridding herself of her greatest headache.

"Of course not," Mr. Wheadon whispered, head hanging between his shoulders. "I will do whatever is necessary to make this right."

"Very well, then! You and Felicity shall marry as soon as the banns are read," the viscountess announced.

Felicity stared blankly at the floor. Could this truly be happening to her?

Did she have any right to be surprised? How often had her mother, her governess, even her friends and sister, told her that she could very well find herself in true peril if she acted out at the wrong time with the wrong audience?

Surely, that Lady Swan could take part of the blame. If the anonymous matchmaker had not infiltrated the minds of all of Felicity's companions—of Felicity herself—perhaps she would not have spared Mr. Atticus Wheadon a second glance upon his arrival in Bainbridge, would not have cared if he'd left the ballroom in a rush, would have not followed him here.

Surely, even if she had meddled, Lady Swan could not have meant for it to unfold like *this*.

CHAPTER SIX

A TTICUS'S EYES GLAZED over as he read his name and Miss Reeve's next to each other, printed in solid, black letters. Permanent and unchangeable. Recorded in the newspaper, their engagement was now real.

His stomach churned. His heart beat erratically, sure to leave bruises on the interior of his ribcage.

The newspaper flew out of his frozen hand, snatched by Miss Reeve. She threw herself into the chair beside Atticus with a groan. Miss Mercy shook her head at her twin's colorful antics, even though they were quite alone in Setherwell's drawing room.

Door ajar, of course, while Mama and Papa took Lord and Lady Eldmar to admire the house and grounds—to leave the young folks to their happy plans, as Mama had said.

In the somber shadows of the library, Atticus, Miss Reeve, Miss Mercy, and Lady Eldmar had all agreed that no one else need learn the truth of the impetus behind their sudden betrothal. Not even Atticus's parents. He had felt relieved and guilty in equal measure when Mama and Papa had proven so ecstatic about any match for their son that they had not stopped celebrating long enough to question its remarkable swiftness.

"It is official, then," Miss Reeve grumbled into the tense silence. "We are…engaged."

Miss Mercy cleared her throat and offered an apologetic smile to Atticus, trying, no doubt, to be mindful on her sister's behalf not to offend the family that would soon be forever tied to theirs.

"Many young ladies would give much to be in your position," she reminded her sister quietly.

Avoiding his gaze, Atticus's future wife scoffed. "Then let them, and leave me alone."

In fact, Miss Reeve's eyes had not landed directly on Atticus since she and her family had arrived.

Miss Mercy's cheeks colored. "That is quite enough, sister."

To Atticus's surprise, the other lady did shrink a little. She recovered quickly. Atticus would have thought he had imagined her embarrassment had he not already been observing her. Stubbornly fixing her frown, she turned her head sharply and glared out the window.

Just as Miss Mercy began to apologize again, Atticus held up one hand. "There is no need. Miss Reeve has every right to her feelings. It is quite an unexpected situation and I shall take no offense to anything she deems necessary to say about the matter."

Miss Reeve turned again. For the first time since their arrival, Atticus's intended looked at him. Her deep-brown eyes narrowed in what looked to be anger and determination as they observed each other for a long moment, lips trembling with fear.

Atticus's frantic heart sputtered to a stop and plummeted to depths he had not thought possible. He was the cause of that pain and fear. *He* had done this to her.

The pieces had become clearer to Atticus after the night in the library. Had it truly only been two nights ago? For whatever reason, Miss Reeve did not wish to marry. Or she at least held extremely specific standards and ideals that had presented a challenge for her mother to match.

Atticus had forced this poor creature into a life she did not want. He would happily accept her insults. He deserved them.

"What an uncommon man," Miss Reeve said under her breath, likely not intending for Atticus to hear.

But he *had* heard. There was no bite in her voice now. Instead, it sounded almost like...awe. A strange mixture of incredulity and longing seized him. Atticus had never been more sure that there was nothing about him to inspire anything resembling awe. But, for the first time in a long time, he wished there were.

"What an excellent tour, Mrs. Wheadon!" Lady Eldmar's voice rang just outside the drawing room door.

Miss Reeve quickly fixed her posture and countenance and busied herself with the now-lukewarm tea her sister had prepared, which she had thus far ignored. She seemed to think better of increasing her mother's ire since that fateful night.

"I do hope you have found everything to your satisfaction, my lady," said Mama as both sets of parents entered. "Dearest Miss Reeve shall want for nothing here! I cannot tell you how eagerly I have been waiting to guide a new daughter as she puts into practice all of her excellent education in being mistress of a household."

"She will benefit greatly from your wise counsel, I have no doubt," the viscountess replied, her words dripping with purposeful sweetness. Lord Eldmar absentmindedly nodded his agreement as Papa led him to the sofa in the middle of the room, musing about an article in the morning's paper.

Atticus had not thought anything particular about either Lord Eldmar or Lady Eldmar during their first meeting, prior to the disparaging remarks he'd heard at the welcome luncheon. That event had certainly changed the course of his opinion on one of them.

After the library, after witnessing her callous, opportunistic treatment of her daughter—where other mothers might have wept with heartbreak or even displayed a fit of anger—Atticus would never see or hear anything in Lady Eldmar's behavior and speech but her self-serving singlemindedness. Even stumbling upon her youngest children involved in a ruinous situation had not altered the viscountess's eagerness to achieve her goal.

As if summoned by Atticus's uncharacteristically critical thoughts, Miss Reeve's mother approached the trio seated by the window. Her gaze never left the eldest twin, not even when the younger rose from her seat and hurried away.

"You should be entertaining your intended, Felicity," she snipped quietly as a dainty hand landed upon her target's shoulder, the picture of motherly pride.

"Yes, Mother," Miss Reeve said through gritted teeth.

Just as quickly as she'd arrived, the viscountess disappeared, striding toward Mama and Miss Mercy by the fireplace, where they admired a small, pearl-inlaid table.

Atticus did the only thing he could conceive of to appease his future mother-in-law. He leaned over the arm of his chair toward Miss Reeve. The lady's eyes widened in a silent question. She did not attempt to retreat from the sudden intimacy.

"You need not respond. We may simply pretend to converse," Atticus whispered. This close, his eyes were in danger of spending too much time on the subtle curves of her pink mouth.

"Perhaps I might recount the book I have most recently finished reading," he suggested, "and perhaps you might nod along or make some thoughtful sound. You need not truly listen if you do not wish. Just so your mother does not find further reason to punish you."

Miss Reeve narrowed her eyes at Atticus and made no reply. He bit the inside of his cheek. Had he said too much? Taken too many liberties? She would soon be Atticus's bride, but that did not mean they knew anything more about each other than they had two days ago. He had not earned the right to speak to her as if he knew anything about her life or its challenges.

"Why are you being so kind to me?"

That was not the reply Atticus had been expecting. The corners of his mouth pulled into a confused frown.

"Why should I not be kind to you?"

Clearly, that had not been the answer Miss Reeve had expected, either. Her narrowed eyes flashed surprise for the briefest of moments before returning to a scowl.

"Because I have shown you nothing but disdain since the

moment we were discovered—when I am the one at fault, no less. At least in the past, my misdeeds only harmed me."

Curls that looked as soft as down caught the midday sunlight as Miss Reeve turned away once more. They brushed against her cheek, drawing Atticus's notice to the dusting of pink there.

The realization struck him hard in the chest. Miss Reeve held herself to blame for Atticus's equally unwanted change in his comfortable life. The brick of guilt that had occupied the depths of his stomach these past two days grew heavier by a hundred-fold. That his future wife should feel any blame for these unfortunate circumstances was a tragedy all its own.

Atticus bowed his head. He could no longer bear to look at her. Why had he not more firmly insisted that she leave the library immediately? Why had he not left himself at her first refusal?

Against his wishes, Atticus's mind brought forth the already hazy memories of that night. It had all happened too quickly for any of it to imprint details. Only one had mattered that night. That he would do the gentlemanly thing and marry Miss Reeve for her protection. It was the least he could do after causing such a mess.

And no matter what Miss Reeve thought, Atticus was the true cause. If he could have simply maintained control of himself and his emotions in the ballroom, Miss Reeve would have had no need to follow him to this great misfortune.

Yet, no matter how often Atticus dwelled in the despair of those moments, he could not help recalling Miss Reeve's tenderness. After a lifetime of pitying whispers behind his back and disinterested replies to his attempted conversations, it had been too tempting to accept kindness from a stranger.

His cowardice had cost him his beloved future of solitude and her the independent dreams of a wild heart.

Could he not at least now muster a modicum of bravery to address the woman who would be his life partner? The silence had gone on too long. He could never tell when the right time had arrived to break it. The right time hardly mattered now.

"I assure you that your disdain and any resulting actions are entirely justified in my eyes," he began without lifting his head. "I understand very well that I am the last man any young lady would willingly—"

"It is not you."

Atticus jolted, his head flying up.

"At least, you are not the sole cause of my disinclination toward this union," she hurried, her gaze fixed on some distant point. "As you might have gathered, I am disinclined toward marriage as a whole."

"May I know your reasoning?" Atticus asked quietly. The more he learned of his future bride, the easier it would be for him to avoid saying or doing anything that might increase her regret.

Miss Reeve's mouth tugged to one side. "I am sure you can see by now why my nature renders me unsuitable for the stifling standards of a wife. And why the viscountess seized the opportunity to force me into marriage. I value my freedom too greatly to welcome anyone who openly seeks to deprive me of it. That is why I had planned to live with Mercy or one of our friends when they eventually married. We all promised we would take each other should the need arise. I know I will only ever be free in a house where I have the love and understanding of a true friend."

Atticus's battered heart sank even lower. "I understand. I am so terribly, terribly sorry for all of this."

A featherlight touch graced Atticus's arm. It was gone so quickly, he wondered if he'd merely imagined it until Miss Reeve spoke.

"You have done nothing that necessitates an apology," she said, still looking away and blushing. "You are just as trapped as I am, after all. I cannot imagine this is how you thought you would be induced to make an offer, if you ever wished to do so at all." Miss Reeve paused, wrinkling her nose as she took a deep inhale, readying herself to continue.

"Perpetually unmarried gentlemen are merely called 'confirmed bachelors,' while unwed women are branded 'spinsters.' What an odious word, 'spinster'! As if it is meant to be insulting, a mark of tragic failure."

The more Miss Reeve spoke on the absurdity of the different rules governing men and women, the more passionate she became. Atticus's own self-pity retreated to the back of his mind as he listened, finding himself nodding along in genuine agreement.

She conveyed her ideas in the spontaneous flow of speech even more eloquently than Atticus could have managed in an hour of rigorous thought. How often had others commented that he spent more time in his library and study than most other young men did in gambling halls? Why should anyone else care if he spent weeks on end without any human contact? Why should anyone care if anyone else, whether male or female, had found marriage unsuitable for their desires?

To hear Miss Reeve speak of her own grievances brought a strange balm to his soul. Though he would not have chosen such strong words as Miss Reeve, she was correct. Atticus was also contending with an extremely altered future he had never wanted.

As much as he longed to commiserate with someone who finally understood him—at least the misunderstood part of him—Atticus knew this was not his time. Even more so as an heir, he would never find himself in a position to depend upon another for his survival. Though it would indeed be a crushing shame to be the one to fail his line's generations of success, no one truly had the power to compel Atticus to marry and produce yet another heir. Not even to prevent scandal—it would not be his reputation that suffered if he refused to marry Miss Reeve. While she could never again hope to show her face before the world, Society would hardly bat an eye at a man's seeming escapades. In fact, other gentlemen—the fashionable ones, so completely different from Atticus—might be amused by it, might more readily accept him into their circle.

Miss Reeve felt her vexation to a greater, deeper, more pain-ful degree than Atticus could ever truly appreciate as a man whose birthright was freedom.

Besides, since when had Atticus developed an interest in sharing his feelings? He structured every day of his life around the one activity that allowed him to escape his own racing thoughts and panicked heartbeats for the musings and adventures of another. But Miss Reeve did not need to know any of that.

"Goodness, is that the time?" Lord Eldmar remarked from somewhere toward the middle of the room. Atticus barely heard their conversation beforehand.

"We need not be in such a rush, my lord," replied the vis-countess, glancing to the newly engaged couple by the window.

Those words, Atticus did catch. For the first time, he found himself hoping she was right. Strange how petrified he had been of this meeting in the morning, yet now he wished to listen to Miss Reeve's words and hear more of the feathery peaks and lush valleys in her voice.

"I am afraid we must go," the viscount insisted as he set his cup on the low table. "We are to dine with Mr. and Mrs. Dailey tonight, and I promised Mr. Dailey that I would examine the rare shotgun he most recently acquired for his collection."

Atticus felt as though someone had landed a firm blow to his gut as they said their farewells and he watched Miss Reeve retreat behind her parents and sister, head bowed and expression defeated.

When their footsteps retreated down the hall, Mama heaved a sigh of relief and settled onto the sofa beside her husband.

"I cannot believe our Atticus is marrying into such a respect-able family, and just think of all the desirable connections! See, dear son? I always told you that those who do not seek love always seem to know the instant they find it. I thought I sensed something between you from the very beginning, I swear!"

Atticus felt as though his mouth had been melded shut. He could only nod, hoping his parents were too distracted by their own raptures and exaggerated memories to prod him for a sensible response. Keeping their secret would not be his downfall. The several new layers of guilt—including lying to his parents— that had been heaped upon his shoulders might be. But he would rather crumble under their weight than expose his wife to criticism.

"Miss Reeve is sharp-witted with a spirited manner," Papa added with a beaming smile. "She will do wonders to enliven you, Atticus."

"She already does."

The words slipped out easily. Perhaps because they were true.

"He truly is in love!" Mama cooed, fanning herself with one hand.

"Did you see how downtrodden poor Miss Reeve looked as they left? That is the look of a girl in love if I ever saw one," said Papa.

Atticus's heart stuttered. In love? Love had never entered into his consideration. He was under no illusions, but he was also not affected by them. Not usually.

No woman in the world would choose him to build a life with, not once they saw the perpetually fretful and almost insultingly reserved fool behind the wealth. Nor had he ever intended to tempt anyone to do so, let alone force them. Certainly not one as vibrant and confident as Miss Reeve. She was his opposite down to the last detail.

As Mama and Papa congratulated each other on, now, two excellent matches and the imminent continuation of the Wheadon line, a plan formulated in Atticus's mind.

He could not bring himself to dim such a wonderful light.

ATTICUS HAD WAITED two torturously anxious days for the first opportunity to align his plans with Lady Eldmar's robust diary of engagements. In that time, he'd considered simply charging up the front steps of Huxley Manor and demanding the first available audience. Until he remembered, palms slick with sweat, that he never charged anywhere or demanded anything.

This whirlwind of a disaster had indeed put increasingly strange ideas into Atticus's mind. With only three weeks for the banns to be read, each day that passed was precious. More than half of their first week had already passed in a disorienting blur.

"Mr. Atticus Wheadon," the butler announced into the impeccably furnished sitting room.

"G-Good afternoon, my lady," Atticus stuttered around the lump in his throat, bowing his head.

As a testament to the viscountess's excellent breeding, she offered the young man a soothing smile and nod of acknowledgment, waving an arm toward a cluster of chairs in the center of the room. "Please do be seated, Mr. Wheadon."

Atticus obeyed, fighting to keep the tremble in his hands under control as Lady Eldmar passed him a cup of tea. The fine china slid against his slick skin, warm liquid sloshing. Ignoring his hostess's gasp, Atticus just managed to right the cup and avoid spilling tea all over himself.

His pulse quickened. This was a terrible idea. How could he possibly think that he could stand against a woman with as much cunning and influence as Lady Eldmar?

"What brings my soon-to-be son to Huxley for a private visit?" asked the viscountess as she prepared her own cup.

A vision of Miss Reeve's crestfallen face rushed to the front of Atticus's mind. This was not a terrible idea. It was necessary. A minuscule flicker of courage sparked in Atticus's chest.

"First, since I have not yet had the opportunity or clarity of mind to do so, I would like to thank your ladyship for managing the situation so elegantly. And of course for forgiving and accepting one as undeserving as myself."

The rehearsed speech was finished entirely too soon. In these two days since his last meeting with Miss Reeve, that was all Atticus had been able to muster. Now he sat across from Lady Eldmar's pleased, proud smile without any clue as to what he should say next.

She exhaled a satisfied sigh as she sipped her tea. "Indeed, most mothers would not have been as understanding. But, as is my way, I saw a practical benefit to this match that would serve all our needs—even if some of you do not think as much yet. But you are so agreeable that I am sure neither you nor Felicity will find much reason to complain once you are settled and this drama is behind us."

The woman spoke so nonchalantly, as if the concerns of the two in the middle of this dire situation came second to the concerns of their families. That would not do. Not for Miss Reeve. Atticus's cup clattered as he hastily returned it to its saucer on the side table.

"I beg you, my lady, allow us to end this rash engagement." He pressed his hands together, praying with all his might. "I have seen how undesirable it is to my betrothed and I cannot bear the thought of sentencing her to a lifetime of misery. I shall take full responsibility for whatever reason Miss Reeve chooses to share for breaking the engagement. Please do not contradict her by exposing the truth. It would lead to her ruin, even if I took all the blame upon myself. She truly is blameless, my lady. *Nothing* untoward occurred or would have occurred."

Panic rose up through Atticus's stomach, into his chest, seizing his heart as he made his spontaneous speech. With every word, Lady Eldmar's eyes tightened around the corners, her lips pressed together. By the time he'd finished, her indignant gaze had Atticus quaking internally.

Silence filled the sitting room for a painfully long breath. Yet Atticus felt no temptation to rescind any part of his plea, not when this would likely be his only opportunity to save Miss Reeve from this miserable state of affairs.

In fact, this could not have happened to a worse pair. Two

people disinclined to marry, one for fear of being forever caged and the other for fear of practically everything else. How could any such union truly serve their needs?

Taking a long inhale, Lady Eldmar delicately set her teacup aside, never removing her eyes from Atticus.

"I am afraid I cannot allow that to happen. Part of the blame lies with me, surely." She paused, fighting a frown.

"After my older children have all married so well and blessed me with numerous grandchildren, I became too lax with my two late surprises. Now I must take an active hand in the marriage mart once again, lest this gossip regarding their lack of matches begins to truly threaten me. Besides, they *must* marry eventually. Felicity has spent far too long feigning ignorance of that crucial fact. Whatever she seems to think, there are no other choices, not really. How can she truly believe that she will be allowed to live in another's household, under their shadow? Besides, when Mercy and the other Bainbridge ladies she trails after are all mistresses of their own homes, they will have neither the time nor the interest to coddle Felicity. Why continue to delay the inevitable?"

Atticus looked down at his hands resting atop his knees to prevent the viscountess from witnessing his darkening expression. So it had never been about her innocent daughter's reputation. Only her own. The injustice of it knotted Atticus's stomach. Lady Eldmar was willing to paint a beautiful picture over Miss Reeve's broken dreams merely to remain in the good graces of her friendly rivals.

His hands closed into fists. Mama and Papa had always been eager to see him settled, yet Atticus knew they would only ever force him on a march to the altar if it meant saving a young lady from ruin and her family from shame—the precise situation Atticus had unwittingly contrived.

Whether it originated from his upbringing or his own ideals, everything inside Atticus found Lady Eldmar's attitude to be foreign and distasteful.

That whisper of courage tugged at Atticus once more. He raised his eyes to meet Lady Eldmar's. Even if Miss Reeve would never admit it, she deserved someone to champion her against her mother's selfish desires. If Atticus must be that champion, then so be it.

He was a gentleman, after all. He must be. Even a coward like him could rise to the occasion when a lady's happiness was at stake.

"Please, my lady. I know this marriage will bring the utmost misery to Miss Reeve. Please reconsider for your child's sake."

Annoyance flashed through Lady Eldmar's eyes. She shook her head, patience clearly thinning. "Felicity is only opposed to marriage because she does not know any better. The girl thinks she is headstrong and daring, but really, she is merely afraid of the unfamiliar."

That struck a chord of understanding in Atticus's heart as he watched his laughable plan collapse before his eyes. Perhaps one day, be it a week from now or ten years from now, he and Miss Reeve could explore their surprising similarities and come to a comfortable companionship.

"Simply put, Felicity does not know her own mind," Lady Eldmar finished.

For reasons he could not understand, Atticus bristled. "Miss Reeve knows her own mind exceedingly well. Better than most, in fact."

The viscountess's faint brows arched up. The silence surrounding them threatened to crush Atticus with mortification until he began scrambling through an apology.

Lady Eldmar stood so abruptly that Atticus could feel the gust her movement created. She stared down her narrow nose at Atticus.

"It appears that neither my daughter nor my future son-in-law know what is best for them. Such a shame. You both should consider yourselves blessed to have my guidance," she snipped before curtly excusing herself.

Alone in Lady Eldmar's sitting room, Atticus sat for a few moments longer, his face aflame. The woman had well and truly put him in his place.

Atticus had been defeated. He had done his best and he had always known it would most likely not be enough. It never really was. It had been foolish to allow even the sliver of hope that this time might be any different.

Yet the expected outcome still stung far more than Atticus would have thought. Though he had not told Miss Reeve of this plan, Atticus still pictured her disappointment at his failure. It had been his mistake to imagine her relief in the event that he revealed his unlikely success.

After some time, Atticus could not begin to guess how long, the surge of humiliation subsided to a nagging echo. When he felt enough strength return to his unwieldy legs, he forced himself to his feet. Instead of carrying him to the door, they carried him to the narrow window on the opposite wall.

Immediately, his gaze landed upon the sculpture garden some distance away. Miss Reeve strolled amongst the statues. Her loyal Bainbridge friends, Miss Mercy the only one absent, flanked her sides. Strange how even from this distance, he could differentiate them at a glance by the sprightly walk that could only belong to the firstborn twin. Despite the weight of his own disappointment rounding his shoulders, Atticus could not help the smile tugging at his lips as Miss Reeve mimicked carved poses to her companions' delight and applause.

If he had succeeded in his mission, Atticus would have never again seen Miss Reeve's charmingly fearless smile. His family would have quit Bainbridge and returned to their own home in Sussex the moment Papa's renovations were completed...without her. For some strange reason, the guilty thought ached.

Though not as much as the realization that Miss Reeve would never feel that carefree and happy with the man who had stolen her future.

CHAPTER SEVEN

MORNING SUNLIGHT FILTERED into the vestibule of the church, drowning Felicity's surroundings in a golden haze. It was beautiful, to be sure. The churning in Felicity's stomach might have paused a moment to allow her to truly appreciate it.

But what was there to appreciate about this day? It was only Felicity's wedding day, after all. At one point in time, she had been unfailingly confident that the only way anyone would get her down the aisle would be to drag her, flailing and screeching at the top of her lungs.

The reality proved far different. Felicity stood motionless as her friends and sister fussed over her, turning her this way and that and approving the final touches. All the while, Lady Eldmar conversed in the pews, accepting blessings and well wishes on her daughter's behalf as well as congratulations on yet another excellent match in the family.

Three weeks had provided plenty of time for Felicity to become resigned to the harsh truth.

The fact that she was marrying Mr. Wheadon helped. No, it did not help exactly. Yet Felicity was intimately aware of the fact that the viscountess could have thrown her to a true beast like Lord Cleasehill. Lydia had nearly suffered that fate at the hands of her own desperate mother last Season.

"Heavens, what a beautiful bride you are!" Clara sighed as she took a step back. Her round eyes already brimmed with tears.

"We will always support and love you, Felicity," reminded Ellen with a sweet, hopeful smile.

"You are brave. We know this is far from your ideal situation, but we also know that if anyone can find a way to make the most of it, it is you," Isabel offered, adjusting a few ivory blooms in the bride's bouquet.

"Thank you," Felicity replied listlessly.

She knew she should appreciate their encouragements and optimism, which had been in steady supply since Felicity had revealed her engagement and its cause. Instead, their kind, pitying words only served to remind Felicity how powerless she truly was.

For all her fierce imaginings, here she stood about to accept her fate quietly, meekly. Nothing she or anyone else said could change the terrible course her life had taken.

Always striving for perfection, Lydia continued to adjust Felicity's intricate lace veil as Lord Eldmar peered in through the outer doors. "Are you nearly finished, daughter?"

Felicity swallowed, her throat burning as she tried to speak around her tears. She would have given anything to remain right here surrounded by her beloved companions for the rest of time.

"Almost, Father. Another five minutes is all we need," came Mercy's answer from behind Felicity as she tightened one of the pins holding the bonnet in place.

"Very well." The viscount nodded sharply and retreated into warm, fresh air.

Looking over her shoulder, Felicity sent her twin a glance of silent thanks. Mercy smiled. Hers was the only one Felicity had seen that morning that was honest.

"I do think everything is in order," Mercy announced, coming to Felicity's side. "Thank you all for your assistance."

Felicity's friends gave their final embraces and hopeful prayers as they filed out to take their seats in the church.

"Thank you!" she called after them, forcing the words out despite the pain. It was the very least she could do after all the strength they had lent her these past few weeks.

Only Mercy remained. She slipped her arms around Felicity and squeezed, resting her temple against her sister's.

"I was not certain if I should reveal any of this," she whispered, "but I have some information that might soothe you before…"

Felicity's ears perked. "Continue immediately."

Mercy pulled away and looked down at the stone floor, biting her bottom lip, a habit only Felicity had the privilege of witnessing. "That day in the stone garden when I returned to the house to fetch a fan—just two days after the engagement announcement, I believe—I accidentally overheard a private conversation between Lady Eldmar and the younger Mr. Wheadon."

Felicity's mouth fell open. Mercy did not attempt to correct her, too overcome by her own guilt to monitor her twin's decorum.

"I have debated ever since if I should share it with you because it *was* meant to be private. But watching you suffer on what should be a joyful day is breaking my heart, dear sister." Mercy paused, her expression tortured. "I only seek to ease your burdens by sharing with you a glimpse into the true character of your future husband."

Felicity listened with increasingly entangled feelings. When Mercy had finished, Felicity left all else aside. It was her turn to ease her sister's burdens.

Unceremoniously dropping her bouquet on the nearest surface, she grasped Mercy's hands. "Thank you for confiding in me, darling. I understand why you did not speak sooner."

Mercy exhaled, relief coloring her eyes. "I hope I was of some use."

"You have certainly given me much to ponder. But, unfortunately, there is no time. Though I suppose I shall have more than enough time to think about everything and nothing after this dreadful wedding," she finished with a dry chuckle.

Despite her humorless joke, the familiar warmth she had

come to associate with Mr. Wheadon took root in Felicity's chest. It had been present since their first meeting, long before they'd become entrapped in this predicament.

The man had earnestly cared for Felicity's happiness and had sought to free her for her own sake. Surely, that was worth something—even if his own interests had played a part in his attempt.

For the first time since that fateful night, Felicity could not help allowing herself to wonder if perhaps a life with a gentle soul like Mr. Atticus Wheadon would not be so bad after all.

The thought had come close over the past three weeks, certainly. Only now, on the day of her wedding, mere minutes from standing before an altar, had she allowed herself to face that thought, to feel the fullness of the possibility.

"Felicity, we really must go. Everyone is waiting." Lord Eldmar's bark broke the bride out of her reverie.

She gave her father a sharp nod and he retreated once more, his impatient scowl deepening. Next, she turned to Mercy. "I cannot thank you enough for all you do for me."

As Mercy's eyes filled with tears, Felicity took her twin's face in both hands and planted a noisy kiss upon her forehead. The more proper of the two laughed and grimaced at the same time.

"Might I have a moment alone to gather myself?" Felicity asked when their giggles had faded away.

Squeezing Felicity's hand one more time, Mercy quit the vestibule. She truly only had a moment now. Felicity used it to clasp her hands together under her chin and close her eyes.

"You must find it within yourself to make the best of this situation for both your sakes since your groom is doing the same for you." When she opened her eyes, she called the viscount into the vestibule. "I am ready," she said, her voice sounding far steadier than she felt.

"Very good." Lord Eldmar offered his arm and Felicity accepted. "Congratulations on your fortuitous match."

Her father's hollow words made no impression on Felicity.

She knew they meant nothing to him. She was not even sure if Lady Eldmar had told her husband the truth of their daughter's sudden engagement or if he'd cared to seek the information himself.

More importantly, the reality and panic began to sink deep into Felicity's bones. Until this moment, standing before the double doors leading into the church proper, everything around her had had a dreamlike quality. She had taken part in all the necessary steps without any energy.

Now Felicity's senses were wide awake. Her heart hammered. Blood rushed under the surface of her skin and thundered in her ears. No matter how many times she blinked or how hard, the scene refused to change. Two footmen opened the doors.

Mr. Atticus Wheadon stood at the other end of the long stretch. Even from here, Felicity could see his anxious habits, the twitching fingers, the darting eyes. She almost smiled.

His racing gaze landed upon her. It stayed. His hands stilled and his neck lengthened. The moment he saw her, his entire being softened.

Felicity felt the same transformation in herself. The fingers clutching Lord Eldmar's coat sleeve loosened. Her breathing slowed.

The fears and apprehensions had not disappeared. They had only pulled back just enough for Felicity to find a touch of joy in the day. What could be the harm in that?

It was her wedding day, after all.

THE BUSY WEDDING morning had come to an end. The breakfast had been cleared away. Family and friends returned home— including Patience, the only one of her brothers or sisters to make the journey. And to round out the celebration, a brief overview of the household staff by Mrs. Wheadon—the elder, Felicity reminded herself, as she now bore the same name as well.

Felicity Wheadon stood alone in her new bedroom of delicate, blue walls and white moulding, still in her finest ivory gown, clutching the welcome gift the kindly housekeeper had prepared for her, a lovely porcelain vase for her bouquet.

Once she had made it to the altar and taken her husband's hands, everything after had passed in a blur. She hardly remembered saying those words that now tied them together for the remainder of their lives. Clearly, she must have, if she was now here inside a bedroom in the family wing of Setherwell Court. She was no mere guest or visitor. She belonged to this family. Legally, at least.

Crossing to the window on the opposite wall, Felicity placed the vase on her nightstand and slipped her veiled bonnet off, tossing it onto the plush, four-poster bed. She rested her forehead against the glass, warmed by sunlight. A surprising bittersweet ache tugged at her heart when her eyes found in the distance the roof of her former residence over the treeline separating both properties.

In truth, Felicity and Mercy had always preferred their friends' homes to their own. Huxley Manor had never been particularly comfortable for her, certainly not on the occasions when her parents deigned to visit. With their constant presence since last spring, it had felt even less like a home and more like a prison.

All the same, Felicity had been immensely glad when her betrothed had made clear his intention to remain in Bainbridge with his family, forgoing a honeymoon and the marital property his parents had set aside for him until his time came to inherit the Wheadon estate. Felicity would have her friends for a while longer.

Turning her head from side to side to familiarize herself with her new view, Felicity wondered why it must always be the lady who left behind her family, companions, and home with no guarantee of finding better in her next, significantly longer phase of life?

A knock at the door to the hallway made Felicity jump and straighten her spine. Could it be her husband? And why did her heart hum at the possibility? But that would make little sense when he could simply knock from the door to their shared sitting room.

She marveled yet again at the bite of disappointment when she called for the door to open, revealing the familiar lady's maid whom Felicity had insisted on bringing from Huxley. Hammond's smile still lingered as she stepped inside. Ignorant as she was, she openly displayed her pleasure at her mistress's good fortune.

"Mr. Wheadon would like to inform you that he is in the library should you wish to join him, madam. Though he insisted I also inform you that you need not feel pressured to oblige. What a thoughtful gentleman!"

"Indeed," Felicity agreed, stifling a giggle. She could hear the clipped, nervous cadence of his voice in her maid's repeated message.

How did she already know it well enough to imagine it so clearly? Then again, she had never met anyone quite like Mr. Atticus Wheadon. Surely, someone so unique and fascinating would leave an impression even in so short a time.

"Thank you, Hammond. That will be all for now. Please return to your exploration of your new quarters and continue making them just to your liking. And do inform me if you find anything lacking. I shall remedy it at my first opportunity," Felicity finished with a grateful nod. The older woman curtseyed and retreated.

The decision, as with most of Felicity's decisions, was made in an instant. She would accept her husband's offer. Being at the center of attention all morning had prevented them from sharing a private moment together.

After stopping two different footmen and her father-in-law on her quest to locate the library, Felicity had begun to fear that she would never again find that place that had so abruptly and irrevocably changed her life. Strange that she should wish to return so soon.

The younger Mr. Wheadon was so lost in his book, hunched over and enclosed in his velvet wingback armchair, brows knit deeply, and eyes flying over the page, that he did not hear Felicity enter the library or see her approach his cozy corner.

She took advantage of his distraction to admire the wallpaper of black with Prussian blue swirls and the collection of candles lighting the space, silk curtains half-drawn over the nearby window seat. A gray blanket, draped over the back of his chair, trailed along the floor and a wobbly stack of books occupied the chair beside him. Strewn across the nearby side table were teacups and partially nibbled snacks.

Somehow, Mr. Wheadon's hair had already become disheveled. He suited his comfortable, intimate surroundings perfectly, transforming it into his natural habitat quite quickly.

Tilting her head to one side, partially hidden behind a row of shelves, Felicity sighed. He looked so peaceful, she did not wish to disrupt his reading, especially after such an eventful day. Yet she knew she should not ignore this pull of curiosity toward her husband. If she was to have any hope of a tolerable married life, Felicity must put forth some effort.

She coughed, announcing her presence. To Felicity's relief, she found the interruption worthwhile. Genuinely happy surprise seemed to fill Mr. Wheadon's round eyes. To her equal frustration, it was an even more endearing expression than his utter concentration or his fretful frowns.

He jumped to his feet and bent in a formal bow. A perfect gentleman, indeed, though he continued to stare in silent awe.

For the first time that day, Felicity's smile came without any force. "May I join you?"

"Of course," Mr. Wheadon quickly agreed, muttering to himself as he scrambled to clear adequate space for his wife. A few books tumbled over in the process. Felicity welcomed the laugh that bubbled inside her as she knelt beside the young man and collected spilled books.

Their hands brushed against each other. A breath caught in her throat. Such a touch should not feel so shocking. They had held hands throughout the ceremony and intermittently during the celebratory breakfast whenever their guests had desired to admire the happy couple. What made it so different now?

Felicity's groom snatched the books from her hands, tucked them under one arm, and helped her into the chair. "Are you quite well, Miss Ree—Mrs. Wheadon?"

Felicity felt another pull at her heart, tender this time. It longed to reassure him and smooth the crease from his forehead.

"I am perfectly well," she answered, surprised at the truth she heard in her own words. "I am still recovering from the commotion of the day."

"As am I," said Mr. Wheadon with a strained chuckle as he resumed his seat. "You need not have come if you would have preferred to rest in your room. I only meant for it to be a suggestion."

Felicity's hand shot up. He obeyed and ceased his rambling. "I did wish to join you, truly."

Did her husband's cheeks color, or were the shadows playing with Felicity's vision?

"Why…did you wish to join me?"

Without thinking—the very thing that had landed Felicity in this mess—she gave the truth. "I wished to express my admiration for your determination to be the least obtrusive husband possible. I imagine nearly every wife in history would have found happiness in her situation if her husband had been thus committed."

Mr. Wheadon froze, looking so much like a deer, a paradox of startled grace.

"Husband," he repeated, a strained smile twitching across his lips. He tucked a finger under the starched collar of his shirt. "I must confess the word is still quite foreign to my ears when applied to myself. Though I am sure it will become more natural…in time."

The gentleman paused and inhaled. Felicity offered an encouraging nod. The tightness in his face eased.

"As to your immensely kind words," he continued, "as far as I have been made aware, a husband's first and foremost duty is to ensure his wife's contentment and comfort to the greatest degree possible. In this particular case, if your contentment and comfort are derived from minimal obtrusion on my part, then I am more than happy to oblige."

Felicity could only sit and stare for a moment, overcome by the earnest care in Mr. Wheadon's soft, cautious voice and her increased admiration for his benevolent heart. It was just like the accidental touch of their hands earlier. She could not dwell in this place…not yet.

Reaching across the narrow space between their seats, Felicity tapped the book in her husband's hand, eager to change the course of the conversation. "Why do you enjoy reading so much?" she asked, entirely without judgment.

Mr. Wheadon huffed a quiet laugh. Inhaling, he leaned back into the plush azure of his armchair, grasping his chin, deep in deliberate thought. "In novels, every interaction, every question, every response, it is all predetermined. I can study each scene and come to perfectly understand why its events come to pass as they do…why the people within it behave as they do.

"The real world moves far too quickly for careful study. It carries too many variables that can irreversibly change the entire story in an instant. In a book, I always know I have the option of flipping pages ahead, or even to the very end, for reassurance that all will be well. If only the same were possible in this incomprehensible, nebulous world."

Felicity's eyes widened as he spoke with an eloquence she had not heard from him before. Her heart lurched at the pain and worry embedded in every word. The poor man had been suffering for so long. When he finished, they lapsed into thoughtful silence.

"Perhaps we share more in common than I thought," Felicity whispered, more to herself than her companion.

"Oh?" Mr. Wheadon prodded quietly.

A warm shiver raced down Felicity's spine. He watched her with interest and curiosity and real attention, brows upturned and head tilted toward her. It was jarring. All of a sudden, Felicity felt exposed.

She was not used to such notice from the gentlemen she typically interacted with at her mother's insistence. They never encouraged her to continue her thoughts, instead seeking excuses to quiet her or return the subject to their interests.

Mr. Wheadon lowered his head, mouth tugging to one side. Felicity realized too late that she had been silent too long.

"Of course, what could a sorry fool like me hope to have in common with a lively and charming lady such as yourself?"

Winged creatures came to life in Felicity's stomach at her husband's sweet words. Entirely too aware of herself, she plucked a book off the nearest stack and watched intently as the pages fell open.

"No, I only meant that it seems we both feel misplaced in this world...our fears at odds with Society's demands."

Mr. Wheadon hummed thoughtfully. "I am glad we now have this understanding of each other moving forward. Perhaps, if it is not too presumptuous of me to say, some good may come of this yet."

An unexpected contentment enveloped Felicity with every kind word her husband spoke and every kind attention he paid. Despite the dismay with which she had begun her day, in its place now bloomed...hope.

Her fingers twitched with the wild urge to reach out and grab his hand. Her sense, what little she had ever possessed, tempered the impulse with a sharp reminder. This was still an unfamiliar state of affairs. Certainly not the worst it could have been, but not what she'd wanted. Felicity had never wanted or needed to hold a man's hand for comfort. Why should she begin now?

"Perhaps," Felicity agreed in a tentative whisper.

Without her permission, her eyes flitted down to the volume in her husband's hands. She turned her face away, face flushing. He was reading a romance novel, a tale where a man and woman fell in love, endured obstacles, finally came together and married, then began their happily ever after with a family. All things she and this man sitting beside her should have done, should be doing.

"But first..." she mumbled.

"First?"

"About our marital duties..."

"P-Pardon?" Mr. Wheadon sputtered.

Felicity heard his soft palms fumbling with the aged leather cover of his book. Refusing to meet his eye—not that he likely had any desire to meet hers, either—Felicity jabbed a finger at the novel.

"If you regularly include such titles in your reading, you cannot be unfamiliar with my meaning. I wish to keep our bedchambers separate for the foreseeable future...forever, most likely. Of course, you will be wanting heirs, and I suppose when the time is right, we must find some way—"

"Miss Ree—Mrs. Wheadon," the man interrupted in a mortified squeak, "I would never, ever ask you to do anything that makes you uncomfortable. Nor do I have any interest in any of *that*. Heavens, no. Certainly not. I have always known that heirs were not compatible with my particular life."

Silence fell between them for a long moment, heat simmering under Felicity's skin. There was only one thing to do when she encountered a situation that made her uncomfortable: ignore it.

"Well, shall we?"

She raised her book, glancing at the title for the first time. A history, her least favorite subject. And a blessing in disguise. It would take the full force of Felicity's concentration to wade through the mire of facts and dates and names of long-dead men.

She had reached her limit with these tender topics and flourishing phrases and humiliating realities.

"Ah, well, it is just…"

Felicity returned her attention to the gentleman frowning at her selection. "Yes?"

"It is just, I do not know if it was your intention, and of course I would have no objection if such were the case, but that history there… Well, I found it to be rather dull, I am afraid. I only brought it down to confirm a reference in the novel I am currently reading."

His frown transformed into a sheepish smile, his steady shoulders rising. "If it is agreeable to you, might I suggest this one instead?"

Mindful not to allow her skin to contact his this time, mindful not to allow their eyes to meet, Felicity accepted the volume.

What was it about Mr. Wheadon that had turned her stubborn head after a lifetime of protests? And why did it feel so strangely pleasant?

CHAPTER EIGHT

B RIDAL VISITS. ATTICUS had forgotten about the bridal visits. The tumult of wedding planning and the unceasing turmoil of remorse had wholly occupied his focus. Until Mama had reminded him yesterday as she and Papa embarked with Arabella and her husband to their home—to provide the couple with a period of blissfully wedded privacy, upon their own insistence—that their neighbors would soon be seeking their audiences with the new bride.

His heartbeat jumped in time with the bits and pieces of tunes drifting from the pianoforte, played by his wife, hands flexing against his knees. No matter how he adjusted, he could not find a comfortable attitude on the drawing room's sofa.

If only he could escape to his library—Atticus shook that thought away, grateful the new Mrs. Wheadon sat with her back to him. Her soft profile came into view now and again as her fingers absentmindedly traveled up and down the keys. She need not witness his ridiculous nerves. Bridal visits were for the bride, after all. Still, Atticus did not relish the idea of spending more time amongst these largely unfamiliar Bainbridge residents.

The music ceased mid-phrase. Before Atticus could lift his head, his wife appeared before him, looking down with a curious, perhaps slightly pitying, expression. Instead of asking what troubled him as a stranger might, Mrs. Wheadon cut straight to the core of the matter. As if she already knew him.

"The bridal visits will be a success," she said, her bright voice both reassuring and confident. "Besides, I shall be the focus of the day. Brides are always afforded special attentions."

A nervous hand raced through Atticus's thick hair. "Though you are called 'Mrs. Wheadon' now, most of our visitors will have known you since you were an infant. Usually, the bride is unfamiliar with her new home and neighbors, but I am the one unfamiliar here. What if they turn to me because I am the novelty?"

Atticus's wife sank into the chair beside the sofa and gripped her chin in forefinger and thumb. "The situation does seem rather reversed since I would normally be accepting my bridal visits at Myhill Lodge, or the other house from your parents," she mused. "But I suppose your neighbors in Sussex will require I conduct another round when the renovations are complete."

The clock on the mantle clicked rhythmically, grating against Atticus's nerves. His gaze shot to the drawing room door. "Our arrival has already generated more difficult interactions with strangers than I felt I could bear, and now adding the fascination of a surprise wedding will surely invite our guests to examine me like a spectacle."

Mrs. Wheadon's hand slowly came into view in the corner of Atticus's eye as she reached across the space between them. He froze when she settled her hand over his. The softest smile he had ever seen graced her plump lips.

"I promise to divert their interests to the best of my ability," she said, squeezing her fingers around his. "Besides, it is already my nature to attract attention."

As Atticus chuckled with his wife, he also admired her bravery and innate self-assuredness. They were traits so deficient in himself that he would no doubt illuminate her boldness by contrast, as was her due. That she was willing to help him at all, to treat him with such consideration despite her own grievances, spoke volumes of her heart.

Mrs. Wheadon showed him more clearly with each passing

day that hidden thing he had sensed from the very beginning—that the former Miss Reeve possessed a tender heart under her fiery exterior, even to those who did not deserve it, like Atticus.

"I greatly appreciate—"

Atticus's chest seized as the drawing room door swung open. A footman rushed inside, eyes fixed upon his young mistress.

"The Gardiners' carriage has just arrived at the front steps, madam."

"Thank you, James. Please ensure that the tea things are prepared." Turning to Atticus as the servant retreated, the lady announced with a tentative smile, "We are likely to have a few minutes to prepare ourselves."

Hope flooded Atticus as a thought struck him. "Did…Did you instruct the footmen to warn us when the carriage approached instead of having the butler announce their arrival at the drawing room door?"

Atticus's wife wrinkled her nose, her cheeks blooming pink. "I thought it might be helpful to you to have some time to gather yourself before they barge in on your tranquility."

"You thought rightly," Atticus replied, gratitude swelling in his chest. "Thank you, wife, for your thoughtfulness…"

He had intended to say so much more, and as usual, forfeited the opportunity to hesitation. Lambert strode into the drawing room, wispy, gray hair quivering with every firm step as he announced two of Mrs. Wheadon's dearest friends as well as their mother and older brother, the current head of their household.

"Goodness, they moved more quickly than I expected. I shall tell the footmen next time to sound the alarm at the start of the drive," Atticus's wife whispered before rising and welcoming their first guests.

Atticus's relief that the first visit came from a party including two of the most agreeable Bainbridge residents was immeasurable. Miss Gardiner and Miss Clara were both sweet, good-natured girls and Atticus appreciated their gentle presence to ease him into the exercise of conversation.

As promised, however, Mrs. Wheadon took the majority of the questions and comments for herself, unless a guest directed one specifically at Atticus. He took the opportunity to observe his wife in a state that seemed quite natural to her: engaging with others and captivating them with her unique charm.

She performed wonderfully, because for her, it was not a performance. The same could not be said for Atticus, for whom every syllable must be dragged from his lips.

"Mr. Wheadon, which card games do you enjoy?"

Miss Clara's chipper question pierced the haze of Atticus's thoughts. He became aware of every eye in the room trained on his face. The young lady wore an expectant smile, eyes always sparkling with an inner joy.

"W-Well, card games, you say? I am afraid I do not play frequently, though that is not to say I do not enjoy it or that I will decline an invitation—Ah, but to your question, well, I suppose there is such a variety I cannot think of them all now," he sputtered, flames coursing through his veins. Even his ears burned red.

"All I know for certain is that you had better not claim whist as your favorite if you ever plan on testing yourself against me," Mrs. Wheadon chimed in airily with an effortless smile. "My friends already know what you will learn in time, husband, which is that I am terribly competitive."

"Oh, *terribly* competitive." Miss Gardiner giggled behind a gloved hand.

"I-Is that so?" he dared to prod.

"You have never seen such a thing, I swear!" Miss Clara added, shaking her head. Her mother and older brother both offered their agreement, the former amused and the latter apparently adrift in his own thoughts.

"Felicity won *one* game of whist against Lydia last Season and would not let any of us forget for the remainder of it!" the younger Gardiner sister continued with a pout, earning laughs from them all, Atticus included.

All the while, as much as Atticus tried not to pay any mind, Mrs. Wheadon's eyes remained anchored to him. Her smile, warm and inviting, reminded Atticus that he could join at any time. It was a testament to both her natural sociability and her growing understanding of Atticus's temperament and needs. She did all of this for him despite the pain she felt at this unwanted life that had been forced upon her.

Atticus accepted his wife's invitation. Slowly relaxing, he began earnestly engaging in the conversation with increasing ease and enjoyment. To his pleasant surprise, it allowed him yet another angle from which to appreciate Mrs. Wheadon thriving, making others smile and laugh while unabashedly expressing herself.

Throughout the rest of the day, the remainder of Mrs. Wheadon's friends and their families came to congratulate the couple yet again and inquire after their marital paradise.

At least, the young ladies did a remarkable job assisting Atticus and Mrs. Wheadon in creating the *illusion* of marital paradise. He had not forbidden her from sharing the truth with them so long as she trusted them with every fiber of her being. Mrs. Wheadon had assured him she did. That was enough for Atticus.

Interspersed throughout their welcome visits came those from farther afield in the area. Though Atticus never reached a level of true comfort, he was pleasantly surprised to find that he felt more at ease than he normally would. He credited that entirely to his wife's valiant, and thus far successful, efforts.

"We are nearly finished." The lady inhaled and exhaled deeply as the door closed behind yet another guest.

"For that, I am grateful." Atticus sighed, also catching his breath, though he looked far more ragged compared to Mrs. Wheadon. She was radiant with invigoration.

"Mrs. Cullham's gig has just arrived at the end of the drive," a footman announced far too soon.

Atticus's anxiety surged when Mrs. Wheadon grimaced. "Mrs. Cullham has been widowed for nearly three decades now and prefers the company of the other older ladies with grown children. She does not often make appearances at the principal families' events, yet somehow, she still manages to learn and share all Bainbridge's gossip."

"Oh, dear..." Atticus whispered, swallowing hard. Since the elderly woman had not yet been introduced to Atticus, she might find him of particular interest.

"Fear not, Mr. Wheadon," his wife replied firmly with an encouraging glint in her eyes. "We shall overcome together."

Mrs. Wheadon's warning proved extremely useful to Atticus's rattled nerves. The widow was indeed as voluble as she was inquisitive from the moment she stepped a diminutive, dainty foot inside the drawing room. Gesturing enthusiastically, she launched into greetings and congratulations as well as bits of advice and questions as she crossed to join her hosts. Atticus and Mrs. Wheadon exchanged a commiserating glance.

"How lovely of you to visit, Mrs. Cullham. Please do be seated," Mrs. Wheadon managed to interject as the older woman finally drew breath.

"I rather like the look of this seat just here."

To Atticus's dismay, their guest perched on the sofa beside him with a prim huff. She smoothed her dark-purple skirts and craned her neck to peer up at Atticus, narrowing her watery, blue eyes.

"Yes, I should like to take a good look at the handsome, romantic young man who so quickly swept one of our most stubborn misses off her feet," Mrs. Cullham continued in a tone that indicated she knew more than anyone about the new Mr. and Mrs. Wheadon, including them.

Atticus's muscles seized, preparing to catapult him through the ceiling if necessary. "Y-You are too kind, madam," he mumbled.

"My dear husband is too modest, is he not?" Mrs. Wheadon offered quickly, taking the chair she had intended for their guest and leaning as far forward as possible to force the woman's attention in her direction.

Though Atticus longed to object, he understood his wife's tactic. If Mrs. Cullham sought something tantalizing enough to report through her circle, they must deliver.

Mrs. Cullham turned to her hostess, scrunching her nose. "Modest? A gentleman with height and a pleasing figure, modest? I am sure I know fellows with far less to recommend them than your Mr. Wheadon who act as though they have never encountered the word."

"Indeed! Mr. Wheadon is quite a rarity in many regards, in fact. I have never met such an intelligent, well-read man who places such high value on pursuits of the mind as a means to strengthening the spirit. Should you ever find yourself in need of a rare volume, my husband is sure to have it in his library or else know the precise means of acquiring it. And his thoughtfulness and consideration!"

The outpouring of compliments from Atticus's wife achieved the goal of distracting Mrs. Cullham from driving him to insanity with her probing questions. Mrs. Wheadon wove morsels of information throughout her praises that the other woman inhaled with immense interest. Atticus only had to offer the occasional word of agreement to appear engaged.

However, Mrs. Wheadon's surprisingly robust list of Atticus's fine qualities achieved another unintended result. With each word his wife spoke, Atticus felt himself willfully forgetting that, in truth, any compliments she paid him were lies. They only existed to bolster the deception of their felicitous marriage. He felt himself entertaining the hope that perhaps these lies carried the potential for truth...someday.

"Well, I must say I have never seen a truly happy pair so opposite in temperament," Mrs. Cullham announced after a long thirty or so minutes, nodding her approval at Atticus and Mrs. Wheadon in turn.

To Atticus's surprise, Mrs. Wheadon's expression tightened. "Surely, you have not already forgotten the young Harrowsmiths simply because they are no longer the most recent marriage," she said with a light chuckle. Her usually generous smile no longer reached her eyes. "If they are happy, there is no reason why Mr. Wheadon and I should not also be happy."

Atticus stared at his wife. Why couldn't her words be true? The mere possibility was enough to awaken a glimmer of courage.

"I very much agree with Mrs. Wheadon," he said, his gravelly voice solidifying as he spoke. "How could I not be overjoyed with such a spirited, open, understanding wife? I knew from the moment of our first meeting that she was unlike anyone I had ever met... Her heart heard the language spoken only by my own."

When he'd finished his own speech, Atticus could not fathom what had possessed him to say such uncommonly bold and dreadfully flowery things. Both ladies watched him with impressed expressions. Mrs. Cullham grudgingly nodded to herself while Mrs. Wheadon wore a warm, proud smile, her chin lifted.

Proud? Of him? Not likely, Atticus reminded himself. Mrs. Wheadon had revealed quite a talent for masking her true circumstances and feelings over the course of the day. The light in her eyes, the slightly parted lips, the increased speed of her breath... All part of the act. If Atticus was so sure of it, why did his heart hum in response?

"Charming, indeed," Mrs. Cullham said, satisfaction coloring her raspy voice as she rose from her seat.

"Bainbridge is blessed to have two such merry unions in such short order! Now, I am never one to dawdle, so I am afraid I must leave you poor young people to manage all on your own. Ah! But I suppose that is how it was when I first married my dearly departed Mr. Cullham. Still, I should have liked to have had the wisdom of a markedly older neighbor to ease the transition of those early days and weeks. Not that six-and-seventy can be considered markedly old these days, mind you—"

The couple nodded along in unison as they accompanied their last guest to the drawing room doors and gratefully accepted her assurances of another visit just as soon as she was able, though it might take rather longer than they would like, for her engagement diary always seemed to have just so many claims upon it.

As a footman closed the door behind the woman, Mrs. Wheadon propped both fists on her hips in a powerful stance. She whirled around to face Atticus, who had been content to remain a few steps behind his wife.

A triumphant smile brought her face to life in a way Atticus had not yet witnessed. The hum in his heart increased in intensity. Perhaps they had indeed developed some sort of language between them. Not one of love, but one of necessity.

"We did it, Mr. Wheadon! We survived the first day of our bridal visit battles, and whatever remains shall not be nearly as challenging. You performed admirably."

"As did you," Atticus replied, unable to muster more than a whisper.

Mrs. Wheadon shook her head. "Such social obligations have never caused me much suffering. This victory was entirely your own."

She gestured toward Atticus with both hands, palms up. For a strange, wild moment, the desire to take hold of them for a very, very long time surged through Atticus's veins.

"I would much rather share the sweetness of victory with my wife."

After a moment of silence, Mrs. Wheadon finally answered, "I would like that. And what better way to celebrate than with sweets?"

As she crossed to the service bell and pulled, Atticus returned to his seat in a daze. If they continued like this, there was no knowing what else they might come to share with each other.

CHAPTER NINE

E VERY MUSCLE IN Felicity's body twitched with apprehension—particularly her fingers, enclosed as they were by her husband's hand. Late-morning sunlight, diluted by gray-tinged clouds, penetrated the darkness behind her closed lids.

As Felicity had finished breakfast in her bedroom, as she always did—one of the few advantages of being a married woman, she'd found—Hammond had informed her that Mr. Wheadon requested her presence in the back foyer, dressed for a walk. Never in their month of marriage had he made a request rather than a suggestion. When she had arrived and at every subsequent query, Mr. Wheadon refused to inform her of their destination or purpose.

Though Felicity loved surprises, she owed the sputters in her heart to a different source. Mr. Wheadon's fingers squeezed as he led her across the trimmed lawn.

"We are nearly there."

Felicity could only swallow and nod, too focused on the sensation of their joined hands. It was the boldest display of affection her husband had offered thus far despite growing closer and learning pieces about each other's interests and histories over the past month.

Not that she had been particularly encouraging, Felicity admitted to herself.

In those first few days after their engagement, when the rage and despair were at their freshest, Felicity had been so certain that she would never desire anything to do with her husband, no matter how soft-spoken and kind.

Now she found herself reveling in the feeling of his hand around hers, a late-summer breeze laced with a faint aroma, and the promise of a surprise before her.

A moment later, Mr. Wheadon released Felicity's hand and came to a stop. The hint of impending chill in the air cut straight through her at the sudden removal of his closeness.

Almost in the same instant, a column of steam raced from the base of her spine all the way up to her face as he instead came to stand behind her. Felicity's back brushed against her husband's firm chest with her next inhale. His arms encircled her and her mind went blank. Large hands hovered just over her closed eyes, so close, Felicity swore she could feel them on her skin.

"I once read in a book that a delay of a few seconds will create greater suspense," he whispered into her ear. If he felt the tendons in her neck tightening or the heat rising to her cheeks, he feigned his ignorance exceedingly well.

Urgent pleas balanced on the edge of Felicity's tongue, on the verge of tipping across the threshold of her lips and demanding that the gentleman release her. In one month of marriage, they had never stood this close before. How was Felicity to endure it even for a few seconds?

"Here we are," Mr. Wheadon cried just when Felicity thought her mind would break, throwing his hands into the air and stepping back.

Felicity's heartbeat refused to slow as her eyes flew open. The most wonderful sight stretched before her. A grin overtook her features and she momentarily forgot her traitorous disappointment at the loss of Mr. Wheadon's arms around her.

"Strawberries!" she cheered, bobbing up and down on her toes.

Indeed, Felicity had been so overwhelmed that she had completely disregarded that familiar scent she'd noticed earlier—the sweet, delicious scent of her favorite food. Surely, Felicity must have walked into a dream. A giant field with rows upon rows of juicy strawberries, ripe for the picking, could only exist in a dream.

"I am glad Miss Abbott made mention when she called on you the other day that you love strawberries. These are the last of the year."

"All this time and I had no idea Setherwell boasted such a plethora! Then again, perhaps it is best that I was ignorant. Had I known, I would have trespassed here every day during harvest." She laughed.

Another laugh, resonant and real, joined hers. Mr. Wheadon had laughed. It was the only thing that could have distracted Felicity from her strawberry heaven. She spun around just as a gust of wind tousled his dark hair.

"At least you need not trespass now. Each and every strawberry belongs to you if you should wish it...though I do hope you might allow me one or two."

Her husband's eyes sparkled with joy, handsome creases appearing around his mouth, as he...teased her. Mr. Wheadon was actually *teasing* Felicity. Her grin returned. Without answering, she picked up her green skirts and trotted the remaining few yards to the nearest row. She trusted Mr. Wheadon would follow.

The delicious smell nearly made Felicity dizzy as she plucked a plump fruit from its raised bed, red staining her green, lace gloves. When she looked over her shoulder, she found that her husband had indeed followed, catching up easily with his long strides.

"Here you are, then," she announced, chin in the air.

Mr. Wheadon's gaze darted back and forth from Felicity to the strawberry in her hand as she inched it closer to his face ever so slowly. He looked utterly bewildered and unprepared. The corner of Felicity's mouth pulled up.

Just as the tip of the fruit grazed Mr. Wheadon's lips, Felicity swerved the strawberry to her own mouth. She took a generous bite, giggling when a trail of juice dripped down her chin, and brandished the remainder before the man's face like a trophy.

He laughed again, even brighter this time. Every other thought fled Felicity's mind. She had not thought she would be blessed enough to hear his unrestrained laughter again so soon. The warm, full sound and the lighthearted smile that accompanied it distracted Felicity from his movements.

Thoughtful as always, Mr. Wheadon dabbed at his wife's face with a kerchief he had produced without her notice. Protected by the thin, white cloth, his finger brushed delicate circles along her chin and jawline. Felicity froze. If she moved her head even a little, her lips would brush against his exposed skin.

"There," he said as he tucked the kerchief back into his pocket.

Before Felicity could muster a sensible thought, Mr. Wheadon stunned her yet again. The gentleman stole the strawberry from Felicity's loose grip, right before her very eyes. With a bashful smile, he took a small bite.

Felicity gasped, eyes as round as saucers, clapping both hands over her mouth in exaggerated shock.

"Good heavens, p-please forgive me," Mr. Wheadon stammered, dropping the stem to the ground. Closing his mouth belatedly, he wrung his hands together.

She truly could not help herself now. A laugh burst forth from deep within Felicity's chest. Her poor husband was not yet familiar with her penchant for dramatics.

Forgetting all else, Felicity took Mr. Wheadon's hand and intertwined their fingers. "My reaction was of impressed shock, not offended shock," she clarified. "Though, if such grandiose displays do not suit you, I do not mind tempering them."

He sighed with relief. The worry melted from his expression, replaced by his innate kindness. "May I make a request of you, Mrs. Wheadon?"

"Certainly," Felicity agreed before the last word had left his lips.

With their hands locked like this, with his eyes glancing at her mouth, Felicity might have granted any request on his behalf. Gone were her vehement claims that submitting to any man would be entirely unbearable.

But Mr. Wheadon was not just any man, was he? Not anymore. Perhaps he never had been.

"Please promise me that you will inform me immediately should I ever do anything to offend or upset you," he continued, his voice low, his breath warm against her face. "It is the absolute last thing I wish to do after everything you have sacrificed because of me."

Felicity's heart dropped as guilt contorted his expression. She tightened her grip. "If anyone carries blame for this, it is I."

And perhaps Lady Swan carried the greatest share of blame for filling Felicity's head with the idea of Mr. Wheadon. At least during those moments, diminishing in intensity and frequency, when Felicity most bitterly regretted her fate, she found it easier to direct her anger at her unknown matchmaker.

That was far preferable to examining her own long-standing pattern of behavior which had contributed to her rash decision and disregard for potential consequences until it had been too late.

Before Mr. Wheadon could protest, Felicity dropped his hand, turned on her heel, and began marching down the row of ripe fruits.

The constant contradiction of her feelings had been driving her closer and closer to the edge of madness over these past several weeks. Felicity doubted the hot resentment she felt toward her mother would ever truly disappear, yet she could not deny that her general displeasure had begun to lessen since her wedding day.

Was she merely resigned to her new life or had Felicity begun to truly *enjoy* being married to Mr. Wheadon? Or did she simply feel indebted to the great effort he had undertaken to ensure her comfort at every turn?

Felicity shook her head, her ribbon-trimmed bonnet protesting. After a lifetime of knowing her precise opinion on *everything*, she detested this loop of questions and the new considerations each one produced.

She may have continued marching clear to the other end of the estate if not for the hand that grabbed her wrist. With a touch too much force, Mr. Wheadon spun her around to face him. Felicity's booted feet clashed against his. She stumbled into a partial embrace. The scent of amber nearly eradicated all memory of strawberry.

"For you," said Mr. Wheadon as he leapt back, thrusting a small, cloth-lined woven basket at her. "I had a footman leave it here should you wish to collect some yourself."

"Thank you." Felicity accepted the basket, staring down at it, before unceremoniously dropping it onto the dirt path that lined the row. She looked her husband square in the eye. "Why...are you so kind to me?"

She had asked nearly the same thing on the day of their engagement announcement. Even nearly two months since, Felicity still could not make sense of it. Of him.

Mr. Wheadon frowned. "You are my wife."

That was not enough. It was not deep enough. Glaring, some strange frustration building inside her, Felicity shook her head. She took a bold step toward her husband, toe to toe, tilting her head back to force his eyes to remain on hers.

"If any other man had found himself in such an arrangement, he would view me and treat me as an inconvenient accident at best and a vile destroyer of his life at worst. But not you. And I cannot understand why...when you have every reason to resent me, as surely other men would in your shoes."

Felicity's words hung in the air for several heartbeats. The urge to change topic, to jest, to flee itched in the back of her mind until Mr. Wheadon broke her gaze. Shadows of gloom turned his eyes darker.

"I will admit that any lady unfortunate enough to find herself shackled to me would be treated with kindness," he started, keeping his face turned away, though he made no move to increase the distance between them.

Almost without realizing it, Felicity found her brows furrowing. *Unfortunate enough?* How could a man like Mr. Wheadon speak as though not every lady would be blessed to have such a husband? Before she could begin to wonder at her instinctual reaction, Mr. Wheadon continued.

"But I will also admit that I have found myself enjoying and appreciating your particular company. Every day with you has had its share of surprise and amusement. I have never had the pleasure of meeting a more interesting, exciting, free-spirited person. All those advantages help the kindness to feel…effortless."

Pride ignited in Felicity's heart, a natural consequence of her love of flattery. Her mind continued to rebel, examining his words for falsehoods or unexpressed feelings. "Do all those 'advantages' not irritate you?"

Mr. Wheadon's lips pressed into a hard line, his sadness visibly deepening. "Not in the least. In fact, you have begun to coax me out of my comfortable routine. I have not smiled or laughed as much in my life as I have since I came to share a home with you. Mama and Papa have even noted that my letters are cheerier. They are certainly longer, because you give me so many fascinating things to record."

When he paused, voice fading on the breeze and fingers fidgeting with his coat, Felicity tapped the toe of his boot with hers. Mr. Wheadon glanced at her from the corner of his eye. Felicity tapped her foot again, a silent encouragement.

The man exhaled, lifting his head to look far beyond Felicity. "I have already grown quite accustomed to your presence. And, if I may confess a little selfishness, I am glad your vibrancy will always be near to bring color to my otherwise mostly gray life." With a tentative smile, Mr. Wheadon gestured toward the fields bursting with green and red all around them.

Felicity was far more than flattered now. As she stared back at Mr. Wheadon, her muscles loosening and her mind slowing, she realized she was on the verge of being completely enchanted.

Aside from her twin and their friends, no one had ever told Felicity in so many words that they enjoyed her company and longed for more of it. But they had known her for her entire life and, by virtue of sheer exposure, more readily overlooked the oddities and flaws at which every stranger turned up their nose.

Until Mr. Wheadon. The thought brought an unexpected sense of comfort. It would be nice, Felicity supposed, if the person tied to her forever did not hate her...liked her, even.

As if hearing her thoughts, Mr. Wheadon returned his gaze to Felicity's face. A deep, rosy hue spread across his cheeks, yet his eyes remained firmly on hers.

"Might I make another request?" he asked quietly.

Felicity could only nod, terrified of what nonsense might come flying out of her mouth with all these confusing thoughts and sensations vying for her attention, her acceptance.

"Might we...might we now call each other by our Christian names?"

The question nearly took Felicity's breath away. To use another's given name, without the safeguard of titles, was an intimacy all its own. He wanted that with *her*?

"I thought, perhaps, since we have been married for a little more than a month now and have deepened our knowledge of each other... At least, that is my hope, but of course if it is far too impertinent of an assumption—Heavens, this was all terribly impertinent, now that I think—"

Instinctively, Felicity silenced her husband by taking both his hands in hers. She swung them side to side gently.

"I think that is a brilliant idea, Atticus. Nothing would make me happier in this moment...other than filling my basket to the brim with these perfect strawberries."

Atticus laughed, comfortable though not as loudly as before.

She felt relieved to ease the intensity between them. It was not a negative intensity, yet all the same, it had threatened to overtake Felicity's senses.

For the first time in her life, she did not wish to say something she might come to regret. She had always claimed that she would never regret a single word she uttered because she ensured every word was the truth, and one should never regret the truth.

But, with Lady Swan's letter always in the back of her mind, how could she be certain if anything she thought or felt now truly originated in her? Until she was certain, Felicity would not risk saying anything that could hurt a soul as sweet as Mr. Wheadon—Atticus.

She knew she must do whatever she could to protect a heart that had been so accustomed to anticipating pain that pain had become its constant state.

"Please lead the way," said Atticus, sweeping an arm out before Felicity. "Ah, I forgot to mention. This one that I shall carry is for you to fill as well." He indicated an identical basket that sat neatly beside Felicity's.

A wave of pleasant heat rushed through her from head to toe. Would she ever become used to her husband's kind consideration? Perhaps someday, but certainly not today.

Angling her bonnet to keep her traitorous emotions out of view, Felicity quickly bent at the knees and snatched up her own overturned basket before the gentleman could. She fussed with brushing off bits of grass and dirt from it, forcing herself to breathe at a normal pace, or at least as normal as she could achieve at present.

Felicity turned to Atticus, straightened her shoulders, lifted her chin, and offered her arm. "Shall we?" she asked, praying her chipper tone would mask enough of the tumult beneath the surface.

"We shall." Atticus accepted with a grin.

He took Felicity's arm and linked it with his, settling her hand on his forearm and his hand over hers. He kept it there as they leisurely walked up and down the strawberry field, mostly collected save for these rows Atticus had set aside particularly for her.

Everything slowed down around and within Felicity. The storm of her rebellious, temperamental nature stilled. And she...did not mind. She did not grow bored or yearn for the next adventure—or misadventure, rather, as they often turned out. For once, no excitement or stimulation could induce Felicity to break this comfortable contentment.

With Atticus beside her, life had become peaceful. Perhaps she had not realized that she did require some periods of peace and calm until she had no choice but to attempt it.

What else might she be on the verge of realizing? For now, settled into a comfortable silence, Felicity did not wish to worry about all that. Something about this already felt entirely natural.

Against all reason, something about Atticus himself felt entirely natural.

CHAPTER TEN

T HE BREAKFAST ROOM door swung open once more. Atticus glanced up from his plate of buttered toast and cold ham. He would likely have a letter or two from his parents or sister. There had been nothing in the morning post for him the past two days, not an entirely unusual occurrence.

Eyes widening, spine straightening, Atticus shot to his feet. "Mrs. Wh—Felicity."

Framed by the ornately carved doorway, aglow in sunlight from the window opposite, stood his wife. Her inquisitive eyes swept over the beautiful breakfast room, hands clasped at her middle, before landing on him.

"Good morning, Atticus," she said, taking a small step into the room.

Dozens of scenarios flashed through Atticus's mind. Had he ever seen his wife look so hesitant? And why had she come *here*? Felicity had not once shared breakfast with Atticus. Surely, that could only mean that some terrible thing had come to pass.

"Good morning, Felicity," Atticus repeated dumbly, struggling to grab a hold of himself.

"I thought I might join you for breakfast today, if that is not disagreeable to you."

"Of course. Nothing would be more disagreeable." Atticus squeezed his eyes shut in a mortified grimace. "I meant to say, nothing would be more *agreeable*...or perhaps, nothing would be disagreeable that involved you. In other words, yes, please join me."

Atticus hung his head and gestured to the table, keeping his eyes closed, as his sputtering speech finally came to an end. He thought he had been growing closer with Felicity day by day. The increasing familiarity had done wonders to ease his nerves and his guilt. It had even inspired him to surprise her yesterday with an afternoon of strawberry picking.

Yesterday… Much had changed yesterday.

The light scraping of chair against floor broke Atticus free of his thoughts long enough to look up. His wife had taken her seat. Not at the other end of the table, but at his right hand.

"I thought I might sit here," she said as she unfolded her napkin and laid it across her lap. "I know it is not proper, yet I cannot help thinking that if a husband and wife are inclined to be in the same room as each other at the very start of the morning, when no one is at their best, surely, they need not sit at such a great distance. How ever am I to converse with you from all that way? We might as well dine across the Channel."

Seeing her so comfortable, so naturally a part of the room, as if she had met Atticus here every morning since their wedding, allowed his tensed legs to give way. He sank back down onto his own chair and chuckled.

"I am glad you wish to converse with me—though I do often think I would prefer a distance of the Channel when conversing with most people. If I may ask, why did you decide to take your breakfast here this morning?"

Felicity remained focused on selecting her items from the various platters before her. She remained equally focused on her plate as she began slicing at her ham.

"There is a matter I should like to discuss with you."

Atticus tried to ignore the way his hope deflated. He had not even realized that he'd harbored any particular hope when he'd posed the question. After they discussed whatever Felicity had in mind, would she deign to share breakfast with Atticus tomorrow?

Or the day after? Or ever again?

"I am happy to be of assistance in any way I can," he answered, quickly downing a sip of tea. He should not have been greedy. They shared dinner together every evening, primarily alone and on occasion with Felicity's sister, friends, and neighbors.

Yet there was something entirely different about seeing his wife at the start of his day, comfortable in her morning robe and slightly askew cap. The locks of blonde that peeked out were still curled tightly around bits of cloth. To share the morning meal with one's wife was a privilege, Atticus knew. He had never been more certain of that.

Felicity continued cutting her food into smaller and smaller morsels, still without looking at her husband. "Now that I am to be mistress of my own home when we leave behind Bainbridge and Myhill Lodge, I have been considering what alterations I would like to make to our future house and grounds."

"Indeed, anything you wish," Atticus answered, his spirits rising a little at the hint of enthusiasm in her lilting voice. "As soon as I am certain of when we are to depart, I will write ahead to ensure the completion of your desires is in progress when we arrive. What shall be your first directive as mistress?"

"Cornflowers."

"Cornflowers?"

"Indeed." Felicity buried her face behind her cup.

"Then cornflowers you shall have," Atticus promised. He very well might have turned every lawn, field, and farm into cornflowers if she asked—and if their gardeners and tenants did not revolt.

"I did not know you had such a fondness for them," he added. Strange how he always sought ways to expand upon Felicity's words, to continue the conversation, when he could hardly think what to say when someone asked him his opinion on the weather.

"Fondness can develop without warning," Felicity answered,

a touch more curtly than Atticus had been expecting. "Cornflowers are nearly the exact shade of your eyes, did you know? I thought your new home should reflect its owner. Perhaps, if possible, you might see that they are planted within view of whichever rooms I shall occupy."

With her announcement finished, Felicity ceased the overwrought preparation of her meal and stuck several minuscule bits of ham onto her fork. Before Atticus could reply, she paused, utensils suspended in the air.

"There is one more item."

"Name it," Atticus whispered. Could his wife's words mean what he thought they meant?

To his immense surprise, Felicity finally brought her eyes to his once more. She blinked rapidly, her form rigid. She was...*nervous.*

"Setherwell has such a grand library, and I have recently begun to feel it a shame that I do not take better advantage of it. I would be happy to join you there today as well." Felicity paused, her gaze darting away, fingers tight around her silverware.

"Of course, I do not wish to intrude or compromise the comfort of your private time and sacred space," she added hurriedly.

Atticus almost laughed. He had borne witness to a vast array of his wife's moods since their lives had become entangled. This apprehensive shyness was quite novel and unbearably endearing.

"It would be my absolute pleasure to share my private time and sacred space with you, Felicity."

At the sound of her name on his lips, still so foreign to them both, she looked up.

"In fact, I have been spending rather more time outside my library than usual because...I have been enjoying spending it with you, wherever that might be. I have recently begun to feel it a shame that I do not take better advantage of the fresh air as you are so fond of doing, especially now that summer is giving way to autumn."

For the first time that morning, Atticus's wife gave a true

smile. "It seems we have both been positively influencing one another."

"I quite agree," Atticus said, returning her smile. "Now, tell me more of your plans for the cornflowers. Do you have dimensions or a particular arrangement in mind?"

The remainder of the morning meal passed with lighthearted, meandering discussions that began with cornflowers and somehow wound their way to their first memories of tasting Gunter's famous ices.

"I still cannot believe your first ice flavor was *artichoke*." Felicity giggled, the merry sound reverberating through the breakfast room as they rose from their chairs.

Atticus's laugh joined hers and they instinctively looped arms, starting toward the door. "As I said, my older cousin put me to a dare and would have boxed my ears all day had I refused. Such a prospect is terrifying to a little boy... Only slightly less terrifying than the taste of artichoke, I now know."

Felicity's giggle erupted into a bellow that caused a pair of maids by the stairs at the end of the hall to jump. "Heavens, forgive me." She gasped, fanning her face with her free hand. "Artichoke truly is terrifying, isn't it? What a brave lad you were, young Atticus!"

"I will have you know that my preferred flavor of ice is now a light, sensible—"

"Do not say vanilla."

Atticus's comfortable smile widened with every slow step they took. "Lavender, in fact."

The lady's neat brows rose as she looked up at her husband. "Lavender is a respectable flavor."

"And vanilla is not?"

"Perhaps too respectable, which is why no one orders it," Felicity replied with a frown, turning her gaze to the ground as they ascended to the floor above. "It was the only flavor the viscountess allowed Mercy or me to request when she sent us off to Gunter's in gentlemen's carriages. She said it was plain enough not to distract us from simpering and batting our lashes. I am afraid I have come to despise it as a result."

That heavy, sympathetic ache in Atticus's chest returned at the cold pain that hardened Felicity's normally expressive, inviting eyes. The more he heard of Lady Eldmar—who had not called on them or extended any invitations to them since the wedding, a rather remarkable feat, considering the proximity of their estates—the more deeply Atticus came to appreciate his parents' loving kindness and acceptance.

"She has not visited," he started slowly, glancing at Felicity from the corner of his eye.

He could never determine if inquiring when the topic arose would cause his wife pain or provide a measure of relief. The risk of causing pain had always outweighed the potential benefit. Such was always the case in Atticus's mind.

But he longed to know. He longed to understand his wife's heart, even the dark parts she hid behind questions like the one she had asked him yesterday and on the day of their engagement had been made official. Something inside Atticus nudged him with the realization that Felicity might have been hoping for him to prod without knowing it herself.

"No, she has not," Felicity replied with a shrug of one shoulder as they came to the next landing. "Forgive me, Atticus. I should have warned you that your new parents would forget both our existences the moment they departed the wedding breakfast.

"I have never expected that either of them would care to remain connected with us. My mother sees no reason to visit my eldest sister all the way in Northumberland unless Hope produces another grandchild or her husband claims his dukedom. And to think she is already mother to four and a marchioness! As for Father, well, he only had less to do with us because it is primarily a mother's duty to see her children settled. If not for that obligation, I doubt we should have seen the woman again once she'd delivered us into the care of Nanny."

As they approached the library, Atticus slowed his steps. "I am terribly sorry, Felicity."

She stopped and turned to face him. "Whatever for?"

"That you have never known the love and care of a parent."

Felicity stretched her elegant neck, rising to her full height as if challenging Atticus, yet there was no fight in her eyes.

"I have never required it. I have Mercy, and my friends, and..."

Her gaze drifted down. It lingered on Atticus's mouth. Heat simmered under his skin, a different kind than he normally experienced. It was welcome, enjoyable. The hand resting atop hers slowly tightened.

"Does it not bother you?" he asked, extremely aware of the warmth of his own breath against her forehead.

This was important. This was an opportunity to forge a deeper bond with his partner. Atticus could not lose his composure in this intoxicating haze flooding his mind that bore a striking resemblance to the cinnamon notes of her perfume.

"Why should it bother me?" Felicity replied, her gaze slowly wandering across Atticus's face. He did not mind the examination. Her eyes did not feel intrusive. It was intimate, but not uncomfortable.

"Because you speak as though it does."

Felicity pulled away. "I speak factually."

Atticus held firm. He did not remove his gaze. "At times, I hear tones other than fact."

"Such as?" his wife retorted weakly.

"Hurt. Anger. Resentment... Grief," Atticus answered, each word couched in compassion.

Felicity took another step back, their arms unlinking. Atticus's hand trailed down her arm, catching her fingers in a loose grip. He would always leave room for her to flee. Instead, she squeezed, not tightly, but enough to inform Atticus that his presence continued to be welcome.

"What would it matter if I felt such things?" Felicity whispered. She stared up at him with large, beseeching eyes. "What would speaking about them change?"

"Yourself, primarily," Atticus answered with surprising confidence. "Speaking of our thoughts and feelings may seem trivial when there are so many other pursuits to occupy one's time, but it can never be a waste to unburden yourself to a friend's willing ear and accept sympathy and comfort in return.

"Neither the undesirable circumstances of the past or present nor the worrisome circumstances of the future may be altered, but I believe your heart will be the lighter for it. That alone makes it a worthwhile endeavor, I think, even if not always the most comfortable."

Felicity narrowed her eyes at him, extracted her hand, and crossed her arms over the muffled collar of her robe. The strange confidence that had overtaken Atticus faltered.

"Why do I sense that you have not always been mindful to heed your own advice?"

The twist in Atticus's stomach eased. He chuckled and glanced down at his shoes. "Too right you are, wife, too right you are."

"Naturally."

"But I do hope to amend that in the future...with your assistance." Boldness returning, Atticus extended his hand once more. "I believe the library would be an ideal location."

A heartbeat later, Felicity slipped her hand into his. No words passed between them until they settled into the chairs in Atticus's corner, which he'd had finished as closely as possible in the style of his library at Myhill.

Atticus began. "Why do you hide your pain surrounding your parents' neglect behind indifference?"

Forcing herself not to break her gaze, Felicity chewed her bottom lip. "Because...Because feigning indifference is easier than admitting that, sometimes, I do wish my parents cared for me...loved me. Perhaps, in a sense, I am terrified of them ever discovering that. Sometimes I imagine Lord Eldmar's bored confusion and Lady Eldmar's haughty sneer if they ever learned how I truly felt. Nothing would be more pathetic than to claw at my mother's hem begging for her notice when she has made it abundantly clear that she wants nothing to do with me."

A quiet sob racked Felicity's frame. The wretched sound etched itself deep onto Atticus's aching heart. His fingers twitched where they rested against his knee, longing to reach for her. Would it be too much, especially given the already significant changes that had occurred so recently?

Without his realizing, Atticus's fingers acted of their own accord. They slipped across the space between the chairs, across the back of Felicity's hand, until they gently enclosed it. Her cries slowed to a stop, eyes opening to meet his.

"You, divine creature, will never again have to beg for love, for respect. That, I promise you, for as long as we share a house and a life…"

Forever, Atticus finished silently to himself. He hoped that, somehow, Felicity had heard. Based on the flash of color across her cheeks as she tore her gaze away, perhaps she had. At least she did not wipe her tears away, for which Atticus was strangely grateful. She had done enough hiding.

Onto his heart he also etched this sublime image, of his wife, Felicity—so very deserving of her namesake—seated here in his library, in the very spot he felt safest. Most himself. The passionate movements of her hands, the swift transformation of emotion across her lovely face, the light in her eyes when they landed upon him, the trust in her voice as she offered Atticus insights she had only shared with her twin. And when she finished, she directed gently inquisitive questions to Atticus. They became easier and easier to answer with increasing depth.

Nothing had ever felt so right as sharing this crucial moment with Felicity in his sanctuary. In fact, she already felt as much a part of it as the books themselves did. Perhaps it would never again feel right without her in it.

CHAPTER ELEVEN

"FELICITY, THERE YOU are," Atticus called with a sigh of relief. "I was afraid I would not find you in time."

Felicity looked up from her rather creative watercolor interpretation of the basket of fruits perched on the stool before her.

"Look, Atticus," she called in return, waving him into the infrequently used east sitting room. "A little orange bled into my grapes, and now I have orange grapes. Then I thought, why should apples only be red or green? And now I have purple apples."

Hands clasped behind his back and wearing an intrigued smile, her husband crossed the small room. He peered over her shoulder at her easel. "Innovative, indeed. Have you considered green cherries, perhaps?"

"An inspired idea!" Felicity laughed, grinning up at him unabashedly.

Ever since their heartfelt conversation in the library a few days ago—the first of several since—she truly had felt lighter, freer, just as Atticus had promised.

And he had listened so intently and offered such soothing, tender words. He had accepted every bitter remark, every pained remembrance, with complete understanding. Knowing that another soul—besides her sister—acknowledged her suffering and did not find weakness in it...the sensation was incredible.

Could it be possible to feel like this all the time? Seeing her husband's kind eyes staring back at her like that, Felicity knew that if anyone could make such a thing possible, it was Atticus.

"Ah, but you said you were looking for me? You are nearly late to meet Sebastian," Felicity prompted when he drifted into silent thought, a charmingly common occurrence.

Atticus nodded, his dark-brown hair somehow already windswept. "Yes, I hoped to find you and deliver these."

From behind his back, Atticus brandished a bouquet of stunning cornflowers. Felicity gasped. Her paintbrush slipped from her fingers and landed with a faint *click* upon the wood floor.

"The last wild cornflowers of the season," Atticus continued as Felicity's fingers reached out slowly and accepted them. "I know Mr. Harrowsmith and I are to assess Setherwell's grounds today for the upcoming pheasant hunt, but I must confess I thought to—"

"To prepare yourself in advance," Felicity guessed. She hid the knowing smile that longed to grace her lips behind the delicate, blue blooms.

Atticus chuckled and bowed his head. "Precisely. My wife is extraordinarily astute."

"Normally, I would say that my husband is too generous, but in this instance, he has esteemed me exactly."

Atticus's chuckle became a true laugh. Lines deepened at the corners of his eyes and his broad shoulders shook. Felicity joined, their voices blending in surprising harmony.

"Do inform me when you tire of hearing such shameless bragging," Felicity said as the burst of amusement trailed away.

"Never."

That single word, spoken so firmly, jolted down Felicity's spine. She angled her head back to peer up at him properly, curls sweeping across her cheeks.

"Do you mean to say that you will never inform me?"

To Felicity's surprise, Atticus tilted his head to one side in an expression almost approaching mischief. "I *cannot* inform you if I never tire of hearing it, can I?"

The leaps and twists and spins Felicity's heart performed in her chest nearly threatened to force her to call upon that conventional womanly plight of a dizzy spell.

Her husband possessed no justification for looking at her in such a dashing, teasing manner. And when he said he would always accept her silly bravado? How was Felicity's heart, mired in her stubborn fears, meant to withstand that?

"Sir, Mr. Harrowsmith has arrived and is waiting in the foyer," Lambert called from the doorway.

"I will be there momentarily," Atticus responded over his shoulder before returning his attention to Felicity, gaze dropping to the flowers she pressed to her chest. "I found them near the river that cuts through the property to the south. I did not want you to wait another year to enjoy them."

Bowing, Atticus took his leave, fingers flexing at his sides with his nerves. Lydia's dear husband had gone quite out of his way to put his neighbor, and fellow recently married man, at ease. Felicity knew Atticus genuinely appreciated the camaraderie, even if his anxiety could not be quieted completely around his new friend.

A small smile warmed Felicity's features. She would have to find an opportunity to thank Sebastian for including Atticus in the area's gentlemanly events in ways that suited his reserved nature. She would also have to thank Lydia for marrying such a sensible man.

Longing tugged at her, the longing for her dearest companions. So much was changing so quickly within Felicity and she had not yet uttered a word of it to any of them. Not even Mercy. Though she enjoyed tea with her twin almost every day and had ventured out on a crisp picnic with Ellen and Clara two days past, Felicity could keep these feelings to herself no longer.

Abandoning her painting supplies, Felicity raced upstairs, raising the dark-blue embroidered hem of her dress clear of her rushing feet. Barely breathing, she wrote four simple notes and dispatched them across Bainbridge with her speediest servants.

>>>><<<<

"MRS. ATTICUS WHEADON," announced the Abbott family's butler not half an hour later. Without a word, Mercy flew to the drawing room door and looped her arm around her sister's waist, pulling her in close.

"Dearest Felicity, what is this urgent business?" Isabel asked from her seat in the center of the room, her green eyes flashing over her friend's face and figure.

"Did you receive another letter from Lady Swan like Lydia did last Season?" Clara burst out, still bundled in her muslin shawl.

"What is that you have there?" Ellen asked as she neatly folded her own shawl over an arm.

"Let us all take a moment to breathe," Lydia reminded everyone, still untying her bonnet.

Felicity and Mercy crossed to the red, paisley sofa opposite Isabel and sank down. "Thank you all for coming," said Felicity.

Isabel gripped her chin thoughtfully. "This is rather reminiscent of that early morning summons we received from Lydia last Season."

"Have you brought us flowers? How sweet, Felicity!" Clara sighed, skipping to the chair beside Isabel, her shawl fluttering about her.

Embarrassment flooded every inch of Felicity's body. She lowered her head as if inhaling the fragrance of her cornflowers, thankful she had thought to bring them. They would provide a shield for her crimson face.

"Felicity?" Mercy prodded quietly as Lydia perched beside Isabel and Ellen situated herself in the chair to Felicity's right.

How could she say this to her friends when she had not even fully said it to herself?

The longer Felicity sat and stared down into her bouquet, the graver the looks on her companions' faces became. Silence and

Felicity did not often collaborate. At least she had not thought so.

The more time Felicity spent in the quietude of the library with Atticus, the more she came to appreciate its merits. Particularly because Atticus never attempted to force silence upon her, no matter how focused he might be on his own pursuits or thoughts.

Lydia sighed. "You need not force yourself to—"

"I love my husband."

Every eye in the room, already transfixed on Felicity, widened to the size of the fruit tarts plated on the low table before them. Clara's mouth dropped open while Ellen covered hers with both hands. The other girls exchanged surprised glances.

"I-I think I do, at least," Felicity added into the stunned stillness. "I am starting to is what I mean." Her cheeks flamed and she lowered her head into the protection of the cornflowers once more.

"Sister, that is wonderful," Mercy said, forcing one of Felicity's hands away from the bouquet and holding it in her lap. "Is it not?"

"I must confess…" Isabel began. When Felicity lifted her eyes, curious, Isabel seemed to think better of it. Biting her lip, she looked away.

"Out with it," Felicity demanded without removing her face from behind her floral shield.

Frowning, Isabel returned her gaze to Felicity. "I must confess to forgetting, at times, that you did not already love Mr. Wheadon."

Felicity shot upright, scrunching her nose. "How dare you?!"

The ladies chuckled, the tension dissipating. Isabel lifted one shoulder in a slight shrug, her smile a touch sheepish.

"Forgive me, Felicity. I meant no offense. But perhaps our friends will agree to some extent, that the way you speak of him, the way you *are* around him… It is easy to forget the events preceding your marriage. The more time passes, the more you give the appearance of a happy new wife. Is there anyone else who will support my claim?"

Isabel and Felicity both looked about their intimate gathering, each having their suspicions confirmed. Felicity slumped forward slightly. It was her turn to gape in shock. "Do not tell me you all…"

"I suppose, now that Isabel mentions…"

"Only very recently, mind you—"

"Can one truly ever understand the behaviors of another?"

"Seeing you happy brings us happiness, especially after those painful, uncertain days," said Mercy after the others had mumbled their own confessions. She squeezed Felicity's hand, nestled amongst the folds of her pelisse.

Felicity waved her bouquet and smiled at her cherished friends. "I am not truly dismayed, I promise. After a moment of reflection—a skill I have lately begun to develop thanks to Atticus's influence—I realize it is amusingly naive of me to think that I have been successfully disguising my true feelings from you who know me so well. And, truly, when do I ever spare anyone the full force of my feelings? It is no surprise I could not hide them, for I have had precious little practice."

Relieved laughter rippled through the drawing room. Lydia regained her composure soonest and fixed Felicity with a knowing look. She had indeed experienced a very similar journey just last Season. If any of them understood her predicament, it was Lydia.

"We are indeed exceedingly happy for you, as Mercy said," said the eldest of their group, her vicarious joy softening angular features. "Congratulations, dear Felicity. Your husband is a good man in the deepest sense of the word."

"As I said, I am only *beginning* to feel the potential stirrings of love," Felicity reminded them with a firm nod.

"But beginning is the most difficult part!" Clara cried, pink tinging her fair skin, hands clasped over her heart. "They call it *falling* in love for a reason. Nature must take its course. Once you begin the fall, how ever can you hope to stop it?"

Felicity certainly could not hope to refrain from laughing at her romantic friend's enthusiasm. "I am afraid I must be allowed to go at my own pace, sweet Clara. The thought has only just crossed my mind this morning. Well, as a real thought...not as a feeling for which I could find some other rationalization."

"This morning?" Mercy asked. "What occurred this morning?"

Looking down at the lovely, little wild cornflowers, Felicity flushed yet again. "You will all think me mad for demanding an immediate audience over such a small thing."

"When it comes to love, nothing can be small," said Ellen softly, brown curls perfectly framing her heart-shaped face. "Love elevates the ordinary and expands the limits of that which the human spirit believes itself capable. Therefore, nothing done in love can ever be small."

The elder Gardiner sister finished with a deep inhale. They observed their quietest companion with tender admiration.

Felicity broke the silence with an awed chuckle. "Heavens, when did my friends become such poets and philosophers?"

"Ellen is correct," Isabel added. "You are at liberty to share with us, Felicity—but only if you truly wish. It is understandable that such emotions be shared by degrees when one is still coming to terms with them oneself. You know none of us would dream of judging your heart's path."

Felicity sighed and threw up a hand in defeat. "Yet another fount of wisdom here, I see. But still, thank you, Isabel, all of you." She paused and turned her gaze to each lady for a meaningful moment.

"These cornflowers," she said under her breath, her voice trailing off as her mind transported her not only to the east sitting room of that morning, but to the events of the past several days since their strawberry-picking excursion—which her friends had thought exceedingly thoughtful and worthy of abundant praise.

"A few mornings ago, the morning after the strawberries, I joined Atticus in the breakfast room for the first time. I informed him that when we arrived at our new home I would like cornflowers planted. He of course agreed and we spent quite some time discussing my vision for the addition. And earlier today, he delivered these to me."

Felicity paused once more and smiled down at the blue blooms that were so much like looking into her husband's eyes. "He went out across the grounds, searching for them. He did not want me to wait to have my cornflowers."

The other ladies sighed in unison, even the normally rigid Lydia, who had become far more open about her love for love since finding hers.

"What a considerate, attentive gentleman." Clara sniffled. She touched the corners of her eyes with the edge of her absentmindedly discarded shawl as Isabel reached over from the sofa and patted her shoulder.

"I do not understand it," Felicity mumbled to herself in wonder, brushing a finger over the perfect, fragile petals.

"You do not need to," answered Lydia.

Felicity looked up, enveloped in a haze of growing certainty now that she had said the words aloud. It was strange, not being in total command of herself—and not hating it.

"There will come a point where all the understanding in the world will not persuade you to take another step. From there on, you must allow your heart to take the lead," Lydia said with an encouraging glow in her eyes.

Mercy's fingers tightened around Felicity's once more, drawing her twin's attention. "But you may do so at your own pace, as you said," she reminded her. "You are so used to thinking one way, it is only natural that it should take some time to begin accepting another way."

"And it does not seem absurd to any of you? That he is so… And I am so… We are so—"

"Sister. Cease. Your. Rambling." Mercy squeezed her hand at every punctuation for emphasis. "Goodness, how many times must I have said that since our days in the womb? Trust in us. We can see plain as day that you make each other happy. There is nothing else to consider."

"Very well, then," Felicity relented with a quiet laugh. "I suppose I should inform Atticus of my findings and discover if he, too, feels—"

"He does," said the Gardiner sisters in unison. Their eyes widened as they stared at each other from across the room.

"Only Mercy and I are allowed to do that!" Felicity grumbled with a teasing pout as her friends burst into another round of merry laughter.

Since so much of their time had been occupied with discussion, leaving no opportunity for refreshments, Felicity remained for one cup of tea and a tart—made from Setherwell's own strawberries, which its current mistress had generously gifted to every beloved Bainbridge neighbor. Invigorated in body and encouraged in spirit, Felicity bid her friends farewell with promises of a satisfactory report to follow.

Atticus had proven himself correct once more. Allowing herself to seek support and guidance from her loved ones did not eradicate her hardships or absolve her from doing what was necessary, yet it did ease the burden considerably to know she faced nothing alone.

"Welcome home, Mrs. Wheadon. A letter for you, discovered on the doorstep."

Indeed, Felicity was not alone. She froze at the front doors and stared at the small, folded sheet in the butler's hands, pinched at the corners.

"Did no one see who delivered it?" she whispered, accepting the letter.

"I am afraid not, madam. Exceedingly odd, indeed."

"Thank you, Lambert. Oh, have Mr. Wheadon and Mr. Harrowsmith returned?"

"Not yet, madam, but soon. They just sent word to have tea and sandwiches ready in twenty minutes."

"Thank you," Felicity called over her shoulder, already racing through the foyer, skirts bunched in one hand and letter in the other, bonnet dangling to one side. She thundered up the wide staircase, ignoring her staff's surprised expressions, and slammed her bedroom door shut behind her.

Felicity flung herself onto her four-poster bed and, fingers trembling, turned the letter over. A swan announced itself proudly atop the purple seal. She wasted no time, tearing the single sheet open, eyes flying over every line.

On her next, much slower perusal, Felicity's eyes lingered in the middle of the unexpected letter. She might have shuddered at the feeling of being observed if it were not so precisely what she needed to read.

"Perhaps you find it difficult to recognize love because you are so accustomed to being shown time and again that you are not worthy of it.

"Remember, not all express love in words and touch. Some pour every ounce of their love into every action, no matter how mundane or insignificant. Thoughtful care can reveal the depths of one's heart more than any speech."

Those words, and those of her friends, certainly revealed the depth of Felicity's heart. It hammered in a strong, steady rhythm. Time slowed. Lady Swan's scrawling letters swirled before her eyes.

Felicity had been certain that, unlike Lydia last Season, she would not hear from Lady Swan again, not with Felicity and her obvious match so quickly betrothed. Much like the viscountess, the anonymous matchmaker had disappeared from Felicity's life the moment she had achieved her goal.

For reasons Felicity was only just beginning to understand, this letter validated a secretly vulnerable wound in her heart. Someone out there had recognized Felicity's potential to overcome her fears and find happiness in the unlikeliest place. Someone out there was guiding her with wisdom, with patience.

She pressed the page to her chest. Whoever this woman was, however she came by her information, Felicity could now begin to acknowledge her skills.

In her stubbornness, she had clung to the possibility that Lydia and Sebastian's happiness, wonderful though it might have been, was owed to a stroke of luck. Besides, all the Bainbridge ladies had more or less guessed long before last Season that one or both of them had harbored more than friendly affections for the other. Could Lady Swan truly be credited with genius for encouraging two lifelong friends to make their obvious feelings known?

Felicity's fingers loosened. The letter fluttered down to the blanket. Feeling both weightless and more grounded than she had ever been, she found her feet carrying her to the nightstand, where the vase that had held her wedding bouquet now stood empty. It came to life once more with the refreshing presence of the cornflowers.

Vase in hand, Felicity walked in a dreamlike trance through the home she shared with Atticus. The time had come to acknowledge that Lady Swan had found their aching hearts and, by some mysterious intelligence, determined precisely how to align their paths.

When Felicity stepped into the library, she inhaled a deep, tranquil breath. It was like coming home within her home. Because she knew Atticus would be here. He was most of the time, in any case, but for today, Felicity was glad to have the library to herself for some time yet.

She walked through the generous room, looking up and down. At the shelves, each volume individually chosen with care to travel from its owner's home. At the peppered marble fireplace that had seen increasing use, a sign of the passage of the time they had shared here thus far. At the snug corner that bore every sign of his presence in its frequent use—tea things strewn about, blanket stuffed in a pile behind the wingback chair, and stacks of books upon every available surface, walking surface included. He had told the staff, more than once, not to fuss with the library until he had gone to bed for the night.

And there was her chair, as she had taken to calling it without her knowledge. Its armrest nearly touched Atticus's. Felicity eased into it. The plush cushions melded to her form. She set the vase on the circular table wedged between their chairs and waited.

"Felicity, there you are," called Atticus's quiet, warm voice after some unknown amount of time. It sent a wonderful shiver down Felicity's spine.

As did the look of touched surprise as he cleared the last row of shelves, wide eyes landing on the lovely cornflowers in their vase. His small smile slowly spread into a grin.

"I am thrilled that you like them."

"I...love them."

Atticus's gaze darted to his wife. He seemed to read the shift in her very being. "Felicity?"

"I love them so much that I could not but wish to share them with you. I thought to bring them here so that we might both enjoy their peaceful presence."

Felicity's husband took a deliberate step forward, then another, until he reached his chair. His knees nearly brushed hers as he turned to peer down at the blooms he had plucked from the riverbank.

His grin, endearing in its own right, softened into that contemplative half-smile Felicity had come to adore as he settled into his well-worn seat. She saw it often right here in this very room, and just as often during her daily walks, which had slowly become *their* daily walks.

Never had Felicity thought she would willingly spend so much time in a library. The hope of glimpsing that smile had certainly tempted her to while away an increasing number of late mornings, afternoons, evenings here.

Thankfully, Felicity never wanted for stimulation of her own when she did pass the hours in this comfortable scene. Atticus always seemed to know what type of books to suggest that would truly capture Felicity's interests. In truth, reading was not half so odious a task when she was not being forced to assume the appearance of a broad intellect merely for the sake of attracting a respectable match.

Surprising Felicity, Atticus adjusted in his seat, perching at the very edge. He propped his elbows atop his knees, extending his large hands toward her. No second thought was necessary. Felicity accepted. Their fingers interlaced perfectly, gentle yet secure.

Somehow, without intending to—in fact, while intending for the very opposite—Felicity had attracted not only a respectable match, but the very thing she had spent so much of her life refusing to believe she'd needed. And now that she knew she needed it, Felicity could not help feeling that she needed it desperately.

"Felicity..."

She needed *him* desperately.

Atticus was the answer to a question which had become increasingly difficult for Felicity to ignore. Perhaps she no longer wanted to ignore it. Despite her exhaustive attempts to pursue only the best feelings, Felicity had never considered that she might be unjustly denying herself the sweetest feeling of all.

It had taken a letter from a stranger and the arrival of another stranger to break Felicity's hardened, scarred foundation into something with which she could begin to rebuild her ideas of herself and what—and whom—she truly wanted. She wished never to return to her former emptiness.

A prideful whisper in the back of Felicity's head told her she should be at least a little embarrassed that the seed of self-reflection and growth could only be induced to take root by such extraordinary measures. But with Atticus staring into her eyes like this, his lips forming soundless words meant for Felicity's heart to hear, she was already losing her capacity to care about anything else.

"Thank you for bringing them here," Atticus continued, each word chosen with care, with weight. "You have brought so much luminosity to my favorite place. I did not even realize that it—

much like myself—needed luminosity until I met you."

Felicity's fingers curled around Atticus's, the warmth of contentment and certainty pooling in her chest and radiating out to every corner of her body and spirit. Meaningful silence stretched between them as they remained entranced by each other's eyes. Felicity did not know how to respond to such a beautiful speech.

Until, all at once, she did.

"I am falling—"

"I am falling..."

They trailed into stillness once more. Felicity saw her words echoed back to her in the depths of her husband's sweet eyes. She knew he saw the same in hers.

Without words, they were of one mind, one heart...one future.

Atticus's hands tightened around Felicity's as he rocked with a laugh. Pure elation relaxed every hard line and crease of worry on his unjustly handsome face. Really, it was hardly fair that Lady Swan had somehow managed to locate the man most likely to stun Felicity's critical eye. No doubt Atticus suited the ideal of many a lady.

A realization dawned on Felicity as her own laugh rushed forth, clashing delightfully with her husband's. She had been charmed by Atticus, even if only by the most imperceptible degree, well before she had seen enough detail to determine him handsome or otherwise. She had been charmed by Atticus from the moment he'd stumbled down from the carriage, nose buried in a book.

"Goodness." Atticus gasped as the comfortable peace of the library returned. "I have witnessed such overlapping speech between you and Miss Mercy before, but I never thought I would converse with anyone long enough or deeply enough to chance upon the same myself."

"I do not think it was chance," Felicity replied, her thumbs rubbing slow circles against Atticus's skin of their own free will. "I think that is simply what my heart does when I care for someone so ardently."

Emotion filled Atticus's gaze. He untangled their fingers and cradled both Felicity's hands in his, bringing them to rest against his firm chest.

"I am honored to be so deeply connected with you and I pray our connection will continue to deepen with all the time afforded to us."

Felicity could only nod, quiet and thoughtful, a once rare combination for her. She felt the significance of the transformation taking place between them in the truest part of her soul, nudging her closer to the edge until she found herself sitting here bumping knees with her husband, suspended in that weightlessness just before tipping.

She felt the certainty of the transformation in the already familiar way he held her hands. There could be no doubt. Felicity must face the truth head on, just as she always did.

After this, any attempts to return to their former relationship would be near impossible without total destruction of the fragile new understanding they had each gained for themselves. Felicity could already feel herself beginning to forget what it was like to let go of him, to be without his hands in hers.

"I hope you know," Atticus began, breaking the long pause, "that my respect for your comfort and peace will never change. We may proceed as slowly as you wish. A marital courtship, I suppose. I have always preferred a slower pace myself."

Felicity was glad for Atticus's hands around hers. They were the only things keeping her from drifting into the cool, gray sky on a cloud of bliss, all the more pleasurable for its unexpectedness.

"I cannot tell you how much I appreciate your gesture, Atticus," Felicity finally managed to whisper through the erratic pulsing in her throat. "It speaks to the selflessness and kindness in your character that are so admirable to me. Thank you for your patience and understanding."

As she spoke, Felicity observed the entire scene as if from

some distance. Could that truly be her, the one always eager to rush headfirst into everything, admitting her need for unhurried time? It was necessary, Felicity knew, if she hoped to make peace with this new part of herself that had only just begun to bloom. Or perhaps it had always been there, waiting for Atticus to bring it to life.

"Thank you, husband," she said under her breath, so quietly, she did not know if she had made any sound. She was certain that Atticus would hear.

Felicity bent her neck, letting her forehead rest against his delightfully soft mouth. Atticus responded, nuzzling his nose into her hair, pressing his lips into her skin, sending her heart soaring.

Every fiber of Felicity's being savored this sensation, foreign and familiar all at once. Atticus had shown her what it truly meant to take her time, to allow something to flourish naturally. Finally, with Atticus by her side, Felicity could begin the wondrous process of appreciating the moment rather than rushing toward and past and through it.

With Atticus by her side, every moment could last a lifetime.

CHAPTER TWELVE

A SUBLIME WEEK passed in which the air became a touch chillier and more and more of Atticus's and Felicity's days began to overlap. He had kept track of each one, adding it to the tally in his nightly prayers of gratitude. Another day spent with Felicity. Another miracle.

Better still, they were rapidly approaching a point where they spent more time together than apart. And Atticus had never been happier.

"Look at us," said his wife, a wistful lilt in her voice as she gave Atticus a smile of relaxed confidence from the chair to his left. "Who knew I would ever find such enjoyment in reading now that you have helped me discover subjects and authors that suit my interests? My governess would not have thought any of this appropriate or necessary for a proper, young lady—only a bored one."

Atticus's own smile spread as he watched Felicity look down fondly at the volume in her hands. How had she sensed where his mind had wandered? How did she always know the state of his heart?

It must have been that connection they had realized on that day, right here in these very seats, that communicated silently between them everything they needed to know. Still, despite Atticus's general inclination toward quietude, he found he much preferred the verbal exchange of ideas and emotions with Felicity.

Though he might sense her thoughts, he never knew what might be released from her mouth next. For one who distrusted surprises at best and loathed them at worst, this was one surprise Atticus had come to need as critically as air.

"And you have opened my eyes to the vast benefits of exposure to the outdoors," Atticus replied. He slipped a bookmark made of Felicity's pressed cornflowers between the pages of his novel and tucked the book between leg and armrest. Even literature so beautiful it made scholars weep could not disengage his interest from the lady now.

"Our strawberry-picking excursion, for example," he continued, mind drifting back to that day—the day when the mutual resignation and cautious companionship that had developed over their first month as man and wife had begun to shift, and quickly.

"A *fruitful* excursion, indeed." Felicity giggled behind the open pages of her book.

Atticus chuckled and nodded. Without any prior discussion, his wife, too, seemed to note the significance of that event in the trajectory of their marriage.

"I would have never willingly participated, let alone originated the idea, before coming here and meeting you. Of course, Mama and Arabella have encouraged me to join them a few times over the years at Myhill in our apple orchard—mostly with love and a touch of coercion.

"But with you, I enjoyed every moment. There is never any force. Many things, even those far beyond my realm of comfort, become tolerable—enjoyable, even, if you are involved. I have also found many merits in our regular walks, only one of your many brilliant ideas for the improvement of my life and the good of Setherwell. The sunlight and fresh air bring a measure of peace to my mind I thought achievable only within the written word. Though I am afraid my tolerance for 'bracing cold,' as you say, is not quite as generous as yours."

"The written word..." Felicity whispered, her gaze drifting to some distant point across the library. "How can Lady Swan be so correct yet again?"

Atticus sat up straighter. "Lady Swan?"

"Pardon?" Felicity's head jerked up, chest rising and falling rapidly.

"You spoke of a Lady Swan... Is she a writer? A poetess?" Atticus probed, curiosity overtaking him.

Over the past few months, especially with a popular wife like Felicity, Atticus had come to know every Bainbridge resident, even if only by name. In that same time, Atticus and Felicity had shared many lengthy conversations about their histories and the people who populated them. No mention had ever been made of any Lady Swan.

"You must have misheard," Felicity replied in a rush, looking anywhere but Atticus. She shot to her feet. "I believe I shall call at Huxley and take tea with Mercy."

Atticus rose as well. "Certainly, but, Felicity, if there is anything or anyone that troubles—"

"Why should there be any trouble?" Felicity interrupted with a strained chuckle. "The only trouble I recall is that Mercy is still undecided on a subject to paint as a gift for Ellen's birthday at the end of the month. I will find you upon my return."

Turning on her heel, Felicity only managed to march a couple of steps before Atticus's hand shot out and grasped her wrist. She glanced over her shoulder, eyes widening when they spied Atticus's other hand.

"You nearly forgot your—"

"Do not touch that! P-Please," Felicity finished weakly as she snatched the book from Atticus, pressing it to her chest. Nimble fingers tucked away the corner of her usual bookmark. The plain corner of a sheet of paper disappeared between the pages as her lively complexion flushed. "I will find you upon my return!" she repeated over her shoulder as swift strides carried her away.

Atticus's empty hand, still suspended in midair, fell limply to his side. He was completely perplexed. It should not have been such a shocking sensation. He had spent much of their engagement and the first several weeks of their marriage in a state of perpetual perplexity. How quickly he had become accustomed to the contented effortlessness that had emerged between them!

Still staring at the spot between the shelves where Felicity had disappeared from sight, Atticus's numb legs lowered his body back into his chair. He had just been delivered a crucial lesson.

He had never seen such a look of sheepishness on Felicity's bold, uncompromising features. There was still much Atticus did not know about his wife, it seemed. Though his mind still echoed and his stomach still churned with that mysterious name, Lady Swan, Atticus did his best to swat it away each time it threatened to capture his attention.

Eventually, the words in his book engaged him once more. Lady Swan became a distant pinprick of interest in the very back of Atticus's mind.

If Atticus hoped for he and Felicity to one day become husband and wife in the fullest, deepest sense, a hope he himself had only begun forming into words—for words, even in thought, carried power—he absolutely could not risk overstepping Felicity's sensible parameters. She might withdraw completely, taking with her any chance at shared happiness. Nor would Atticus risk her individual happiness, for surely, any betrayal on his part, no matter how unintentional, would damage it.

At present, their marriage existed in a very tender state. As much as Atticus reveled in the bliss of this undeserved blessing, the undercurrent of fear could never be eradicated. Even when he read the truth in Felicity's heart when she looked or smiled at him in that way, contentment with a touch of wonder, Atticus lived with the awareness of how fragile it all was.

Their marriage, avowed and signed in ink before heavenly and earthly witnesses alike, may stand the test of time. But surely, an incorrect word or glance or an attempt to produce more closeness at the wrong time and who knew what else Atticus had not even considered could send this fragile thing toppling. Whatever it was.

When Atticus was this in love with Felicity, nothing could be easier than fulfilling her every request. The questions and fears that lingered in the dark corners of his heart would never, must never, outweigh his precious wife's comfort.

"Atticus..."

He twitched awake. Shaking the sleep from his head, Atticus looked up to find Felicity lingering amongst the shelves. He leapt to his feet. She looked just like a dream, ringlets windswept and eyes shining. Yet her eyes did not find his. Nor did she come any closer. The dream turned odd.

"Forgive me for disturbing you," she whispered, taking a step back.

Atticus extended a hand. "Please, stay. I am afraid this is not an uncommon occurrence...another one of my regretful habits. I welcome your disruption—not that it is a disruption of any kind. I only mean—"

"I understand." Felicity chuckled. Her small smile somehow conveyed both fondness and apprehension. "Though I would call it a darling habit rather than a regretful one," she added quietly, lowering her head. Very odd, indeed.

Despite every sense in Atticus's body calling out that something was amiss, he could not help the pleasant glow coming from somewhere deep within at his wife's praise. She never failed to surprise Atticus with her willingness to accept each fault, new or old, that he'd found in himself.

"All the same, I should leave you be," Felicity continued as she turned.

"I should not mind if you never left me be again."

She paused.

Atticus blinked hard. He must have been in a dream to say something so daring, even with the comfortable progression of their companionship.

Silently, Felicity turned back. She stared at Atticus for a long heartbeat, expression unreadable. She hesitated and sought his invitation to continue. That typically only occurred when something weighed on her mind. Atticus reached out his hand once more.

Still without speaking, Felicity crossed to their corner and accepted. Atticus helped her into her chair, tucking her shawl tighter about her. The briskness of autumn clung to her face. She was so alive, so beautiful.

"What troubles you? Did something happen at Huxley?" Atticus began without releasing her hand.

Felicity forced her gaze away. "While I was there, Mercy received a note from Creeves Abbey."

"Ah, Lambert did mention that something arrived for you from Creeves Abbey while you were out. Are Mr. and Mrs. Harrowsmith well?"

Felicity still did not look at Atticus, worrying away at the loose fingertips of her linen gloves. "Quite well, as a matter of fact. Lydia revealed that another little Harrowsmith shall be introduced to us in several months' time."

Atticus's eyes widened. "What a blessing! Their child shall be an exceedingly happy one."

"I quite agree." Felicity nodded. "There are no two better suited to the task."

The initial wave of joy Atticus felt on behalf of his new friends crashed against the jagged edge of his wife's frown. "A-Are you not pleased for them, Felicity?"

She started as if Atticus had yelled or jumped up, her expression quickly softening. "Of course I am. Truly. They…were made for it."

It was Atticus's turn to jolt as she rose swiftly to her feet and began marching toward the front of the library. "My apologies, I am quite in need of rest," she called over her shoulder without properly looking at Atticus.

As Atticus sat in stillness, he found his earlier sentiments strengthened. As close as they had become, there were still so many dimensions of Felicity's fascinating heart with which he had yet to become acquainted.

Unless…

Unless there were some dimensions she hid *because* of him. Because the realization had begun to dawn that some people— like Atticus, with all his nervous tendencies—were decidedly not made for such a noble task as raising another generation. Why else would she struggle to meet his gaze?

Besides, had he not thought the very same thing many times since he'd first become aware of his responsibility?

Atticus shook his head once more, this time to rid himself of those unwelcome doubts. He was stronger now. He must trust that Felicity would open herself in time and leave behind his fears if he hoped to preserve this precious thing.

It would be worth it. It had certainly been worth it thus far. Atticus would do nothing to jeopardize their tender friendship, no matter how desperately his heart ached to follow his wife.

CHAPTER THIRTEEN

T HE BABY'S IMPOSSIBLY round eyes gazed up at Felicity as she awkwardly encircled her arms around him and perched him atop her hip in the same way she always saw other ladies do. His head bobbed from side to side, the entire lower half of his face slick with drool—a byproduct of teething, apparently.

"There, there," Felicity cooed, the warmth of the fireplace at her back. She began bouncing gently and glanced to her new mother and sister as they took eager stances in the middle of the morning room.

"Ah, look here," said the elder Mr. Wheadon from the writing desk by the window, chuckling and jabbing his pen at his wife and daughter. "Those are scheming faces if ever I saw any!"

"It would appear my two years of living away in Derbyshire have not lessened your memory of me, dear Papa," replied Arabella in her light, pleasant voice, perfectly complemented by her swinging, golden-brown ringlets.

"That is because he still has me, and you and I are ever so much alike," Mrs. Wheadon giggled like a conspirator as she linked her arm with her daughter's.

Felicity had hardly become accustomed to their presence since their arrival yesterday and now they were thrusting this fragile creature at her and scheming. It would be a lengthy visit, indeed. At least Felicity found the young baron and baroness to be perfectly polite, and she had always thought as much of Mr.

and Mrs. Wheadon.

Atticus's amused smile from the chair in the corner, barely visible behind his book, was just enough encouragement for Felicity to remind herself that this was an opportunity. In due time, especially now as a married woman, children would be expected of her...Atticus's children. Their children.

She was not yet ready to face that thought, not when she had only just begun the process of accepting her love for Atticus and integrating it into her new understanding of herself. Life clearly possessed a sense of humor to throw Felicity so much in the way of babies recently, what with Lydia's joyful announcement and now a visit from her new nephew. It was as if, now that she had confronted one fear successfully, life saw no reason to delay her confronting the rest.

"Scheming already, though we only just arrived at dinner last night?" asked Lord Hollington over his newspaper, gaze soft as he smiled at his lady.

"Of course the natural inclination is to recuperate amongst homely comforts after a lengthy period of travel, but I have always been of the opinion that doing so stands as much chance of increasing fatigue as relieving it. Better to take advantage of the first opportunity for exercise and society," countered Arabella smartly.

"And what better way to introduce you all to Bainbridge than the autumn festival in the village?" cheered Mrs. Wheadon, eyes aglow with delight as she clung to her youngest child's arm.

The scene of familial care stung that tender spot in Felicity's heart that had always known she would never share such moments with her own mother. In fact, she had not thought it possible for any mother to be so thrilled to see her children once they had fulfilled their highest calling of strengthening the family's coffers and reputation and securing another generation to inherit it.

Felicity started when the boy reached up toward her face with chubby fingers and grasped at her jawline and cheek, babbling happily to no one in particular.

"You see? My little Algernon has already wisely chosen his companion for the day."

Felicity started again when she realized the focus of the room had shifted to her. She gave her best approximation of a grateful smile and patted Algernon's back as he continued to mold her face in his surprisingly strong hands. She should be grateful for the chance to strengthen her woefully underdeveloped skills with children. There had never been a need to put forth the effort since they had never been part of Felicity's plan. Nor had there been much opportunity, considering how infrequently Felicity saw her other nieces and nephews.

"You do not think it will overly tire the darling fellow so soon after the journey?" the baron asked thoughtfully.

Arabella crossed to the fireplace, her eyes never leaving her son. Brandishing a kerchief Felicity swore had not existed in the room until that moment, the young mother gently—and without a hint of aversion—swiped at the baby's face.

"Not while he is with his beloved aunt," Arabella answered, pinching his round, red cheek. "Algernon is quite taken with you already, sister."

"He is the most even-tempered and agreeable baby I have had the pleasure of meeting," Felicity answered truthfully as Algernon giggled at his mother's ministrations.

The younger woman beamed, a smile that was somehow both acceptably demure and fiercely proud. "He is, is he not? If he is already this lovely at just nine months, I can hardly wait to see the fine gentleman he will become."

"Are we settled, then? A trip to the village festival?" inquired Mr. Wheadon, who had already tucked away his writing materials.

To Felicity's relief, by the time they had reconvened in the front foyer bundled in coats and pelisses, young Algernon had lost interest in his new relation, preferring his mother's company once more. Mr. and Mrs. Wheadon had elected to join the young family's carriage, eager to absorb as much of Arabella's presence as possible despite spending nearly two months under her roof. That left Felicity and Atticus to the barouche.

Atticus chuckled after several minutes of driving in silence. "Do not fear. I have grown quite accustomed to my parents' preferential treatment of Arabella during her visits since she married."

The sound of his laughter traveled through his body and into Felicity's, lightening her spirit. They sat side by side on the barouche's seat, pressed snugly against each other for warmth. Her cheerier mood might have lasted a while longer had they not passed the drive toward Huxley Manor at that moment. Against her will, Felicity's attention fixed on the carriage before them.

"Your parents' adoration of Arabella is such a stark contrast to my parents' indifference. They love her so much. They love both of you—even Lord Hollington, it seems. And now Algernon."

"They love you, too, Felicity."

Felicity's heart skipped several beats. She had nearly misheard him. Though they had come very close that day, neither had dared to cross that line, to speak that word, aloud.

"How is that possible?" she mumbled, praying that with Atticus's focus on driving the barouche and a bonnet fixed firmly atop her head, her blush would go unnoticed.

"You are their daughter now. They need no further reason," Atticus continued gently.

The unease in Felicity's mind quieted. It always did, no matter the dilemma, at that sweet tone in her husband's voice. Instinctively, Felicity let her head tip to the left until her temple came to rest against Atticus's.

"I know that does not absolve your mother and father or alter your history with them, but I do hope that in time, you will come to know the parental love you have always deserved."

A snap of cold air made them both wince. Felicity tucked a little deeper against her husband's side—not entirely because of the temperature. "Thank you, Atticus," she whispered. "I do greatly appreciate their kindness and...love. I am sure in time, I will come to see it as such."

"They would like that very much. As would I."

The remainder of the journey into the village passed in silence. Atticus always sensed when Felicity preferred it, just as Felicity could sense when the words had piled up behind his lips and needed release.

Despite this short time, despite the chasm of differences in their temperaments, they understood each other. Of that much, Felicity was certain. What she was not certain of now was the rest of it.

In perfect timing, Atticus pulled the horses to a stop along the side of the street just outside the village and the door of the other carriage swung open, unleashing a bloodcurdling wail. Lord Hollington emerged first and assisted his wife and crying babe as a footman rushed forward with the pram.

"Poor thing!" Felicity cried, not sure if she spoke more of the baby or his exasperated parents, each speaking over the other with proposed solutions.

Atticus jumped down from the box and in two long strides was at Felicity's side, helping her down. "This teething business sounds like quite a miserable experience," he said.

"I never knew little ones endured such suffering in the normal course of early life. My brothers and sisters make it all seem so distant. That is what nannies and governesses are for," Felicity replied as she accepted Atticus's arm.

Atticus hummed thoughtfully. "Nannies and governesses are extraordinarily useful, indeed, and my family certainly employed them, but I suppose my parents preferred to take a more direct role in our upbringing. Arabella and Samuel appear to be emulating it wonderfully." He raised a hand in their direction just as angelic Algernon, his entire face red now, tossed his favorite blanket to the cobbled street.

"They are, even with his nanny at Setherwell taking a much-needed rest," Felicity agreed, her laugh drowned out by her nephew's well-timed cries. "Far better than I could manage, I am sure."

"I am not so sure."

Felicity's head whirled around to look up at her husband from beneath her bonnet. Did he truly feel what he'd said? She was a moment too late. As they approached the rest of their party, grandparents now fussing over the baby as well, Atticus wore a hopeful smile, his free hand inching into his pocket.

"We are terribly sorry! Algernon is normally so tranquil," Arabella, cradling her distressed son in her arms, explained breathlessly, both to Atticus and Felicity as well as the numerous passersby who glanced over on their way to and from the festival. Lord Hollington tenderly brushed the back of Algernon's head with a palm, smoothing his wayward, brown waves.

"Perhaps this will help?"

To everyone's surprise, Atticus brandished an unfamiliar instrument with an embossed, metal handle attached to a piece of smooth, reddish-orange stone, formed into a cylindrical shape a couple of inches long. Arabella snatched it and stuck the smooth end into her baby's mouth.

The sigh of relief amongst their entire group was immediate. Algernon's miserable sobs quickly subsided into hiccups, which then became satisfied coos as he nestled his exhausted form against his mother's bosom.

"Some days prior to their arrival, I read of a character with a young one of her own who used a bit of coral to soothe teething pain. Chewing seems to provide a distracting stimulation," Atticus explained under his breath to Felicity. He did not appear to notice the wonder with which she stared at him.

"Thank you, brother," Arabella whispered, chin propped atop Algernon's head. Though the baby had been the one in anguish, his mother's relief was greater even than his own.

"This is his second tooth to come through," added Lord Hollington with a proud smile. "But, as such, we are still determining the most effective methods of assisting our dear boy. Some of the physician's suggestions have been...a little extreme for our taste. We had hoped—foolishly, it would seem—that the greatest portion of his suffering was behind us in the days prior to our departure. We overestimated ourselves and left his coral necklace at home."

Tugging her pelisse tighter around her, Felicity shuddered at the seemingly endless and complex considerations made by these poor new parents for the sake of their child. Considerations they *chose* to make instead of leaving them to physicians and nannies. Her shudder of pity and apprehension dissipated when she saw the complete absence of resentment or anger in the eyes of both mother and father.

"W-Will he require a nap or...something?" Felicity ventured cautiously. Though she felt entirely out of her element in such close proximity to a brand new life, she did not wish to appear disinterested or uncaring, especially after Atticus had so gallantly come to the rescue. They were her family, too, after all.

"He will most likely sleep for a time in his pram," answered Arabella as she settled the baby into his forward-facing seat and pulled down the shade to protect him even from this cloud-covered sky. Mr. Wheadon, having retrieved and tidied his grandson's discarded blanket during the commotion, tucked the boy into a warm bundle.

With all right in the world once more—at least as far as anyone but Felicity knew—the Wheadon and Hollington families stepped into the uncommon bustle of the village. They, along with many other residents and visitors, walked slowly down the main street toward the square wearing politely impressed expressions.

Colorful flags strung high across the entire square flapped, skillful musicians played jaunty tunes, and residents and local craftsmen conversed cheerfully from one artisanal stall of wares to the next. The crunch of fallen leaves whispered under their boots as they walked slowly, admiring sewn, woven, carved, and baked items of the finest quality. Lord Hollington even selected for his study a grand wreath, boastful in both size and decoration, festooned as it was with preserved leaves and berries spanning the entire spectrum of autumn color.

All the while, Felicity found herself relaxing into their light-hearted laughter and conversation. She felt almost as if she witnessed something private, something that only existed behind other families' walls. Yet the more she relaxed, the deeper a pleasant realization sunk in. They were *her* family, and she was enjoying a scene of domestic felicity on a deliciously crisp, October day.

"Ah, look who stirs from his slumber! And just in time for the pastry stall! Look, he wishes for you to hold him."

Before Felicity could protest, she once again found herself cradling her nephew, his growing limbs spilling over her arms and flailing about for the sheer experience of it. Algernon beamed up at her and Felicity returned a smile of her own as the others rushed ahead, noses in the aromatic air.

"Sister!"

Felicity whirled around. Mercy strode swiftly toward them from the tall, stone monument in the middle of the square, deftly weaving through onlookers, her cheeks as red from the bracing chill as her twin's.

"And who might this beauty be?" she asked when she came within earshot, smiling at the unfamiliar baby. His head whipped back and forth between their identical faces.

"Lady Hollington, may I present my sister, Miss Reeve." Taking one of the boy's wriggly arms, Felicity held his hand up and waved it. "Mercy, this is my nephew, Master Algernon Hollington, and this is his mother, Lady Arabella Hollington."

"I did note your resemblance at the wedding, but my, seeing it so close with my own eyes is something of a shock!" said Arabella in wonder as she smiled at the identical sisters. "It seems Algernon agrees," she added with a chuckle. The baby mimicked his mother's shock, staring for one long moment at Felicity and then at Mercy and back again, mouth unabashedly ajar.

"Miss Reeve, how wonderful to see you here today."

Another familiar voice turned Felicity around the other way. Atticus approached, every step measured and carefully chosen, his parents and the baron following. Felicity made a quick introduction between the baron and her twin.

"Would you care to share my tart?" Atticus asked after he and his parents had greeted her sister. The smile he offered Mercy hardly wavered. "If I had known you were near, I would have brought one for you as well." The once-perpetual tremor in his voice, though not disappeared completely, had become significantly lighter the more time he'd spent with Felicity's sister and friends.

"Well, what a charming group we have here."

Felicity froze. This time, she did not turn. She had never enjoyed answering that voice. It had never told her anything she'd longed to hear.

"Felicity, will you not introduce us?"

She could avoid it no longer. Felicity faced her mother for the first time since the week of her wedding.

"Good afternoon," she said to both her parents as they paused beside Mercy. Almost in the same breath, she hurried through the remainder of the introductions.

"Such a fine young gentleman you have there, Lord and Lady Hollington. He will do you proud as your heir," the viscountess remarked as she offered an empty smile to the baby, refusing to look up just a few more inches and meet Felicity's eye.

"He truly is a delight," Mrs. Wheadon added, unable to resist the opportunity to praise her grandchild, a hand pressed over her heart.

Arabella reached out and cupped her son's cheek in one hand, thumb brushing over his smooth skin. "Most of the time." She chuckled fondly. "Both Atticus and Felicity have been instrumental in producing the current contentment you see here. You would hardly believe it now, but he was overcome by the most dreadful fit of teething pain in the carriage on our way here."

As if to corroborate his mother's point, Algernon cheered and shuffled himself in Felicity's grasp until she realized he wanted to be brought higher. He threw his arms around his aunt's neck and laughed for no apparent reason directly into her ear.

"Is that so?" asked Lady Eldmar with a raised brow. "I suppose I would be none the wiser. The moment any of my babies showed the first sign of crying, I summoned Nanny. It would seem my older children inherited that inclination as well."

Felicity fought her grimace and instead leaned into Algernon's slobbery kisses, thankful for the excuse to distract herself with the noble cause of delighting a young mind. She felt Atticus's steady presence at her back, so close, she could almost feel his chest brushing against her with every breath, a sign of silent support.

"There are others who do not make it seem quite so difficult to interact with one's own children."

Felicity spoke quietly enough that none of the other Bainbridge residents wandering past them might hear. Her new family certainly did, however. Respectfully, they looked away, finding the sky above or ground below utterly fascinating. Mercy stood at Felicity's side as the two always stood when confronting their mother.

The viscountess narrowed her eyes. The faintest hint of color graced her cheeks, jaw pulsing. "In my experience, with seven sons and daughters grown, children are best enjoyed in small doses. As they say, time apart increases the heart's affection."

"Does it?" Felicity snipped. "You must miss me terribly, considering you are always conveniently absent when I visit Huxley and otherwise so engaged you have not had an opportunity to call on me since my wedding."

"Stop this. Can you not see how inappropriate you are being?" Lady Eldmar hissed, glancing nervously to the Wheadons and Hollingtons who, as a testament to their good breeding and sense, had walked a few paces away and conversed with each other and the viscount out of earshot.

Only Atticus, Algernon, and Mercy remained, but it was enough.

Felicity smirked. "They are my family now. They have never made me feel ashamed of my opinions or thoughts or my mere presence. I hold true value to them."

At that, Felicity felt the strong stability of Atticus's hand on her shoulder and Mercy's hand on the small of her back. All the while, the baby entertained himself with pulling on Felicity's curls to see them spring back into shape, giggling without a care in the world.

Felicity prayed the cares of the world would leave this innocent soul untouched for as long as possible. She prayed he would never know the hurt and bitterness that had caused her heart to rot...until Atticus had unearthed it, taken hold of it tenderly, and planted it in the soft, sweet, loving foundation Felicity had always needed.

Pursing her lips, the viscountess tossed her head in the air. "You see? I was right all along to arrange this," she huffed, though she looked far from pleased.

"Indeed, as it turns out, you did me quite the favor."

Mercy's fingers drummed against Felicity's wool pelisse, a warning. They were still very much in public. If either contentious party pushed much further, the whole of Bainbridge from gentry to stablehand would hear of it before the day's end.

To her credit, Lady Eldmar seemed to also sense that she and her daughter were approaching dangerous ground. She smoothed her expression and took a step back, looking down her nose at Algernon.

"I would still advise a nanny. Apparently, since you have had no proper example from which to learn, I can hardly fathom how you will manage all...that." She waved a hand at the lively child in Felicity's arms, his round face slick with spittle once more.

Calling to her husband, Lady Eldmar bid her farewells to the two other couples and pretended to notice some dazzling item in a distant stall that required her immediate admiration. Neither of them appeared to realize they had left their youngest child behind.

The tension that had wound Felicity's muscles into a painful tightness relaxed as her parents disappeared from view. Her arms tightened around Algernon instinctively and she rested her cheek atop his head.

Atticus's hand, still on her shoulder, gently turned Felicity to face him. She read the question in his eyes and offered a tight smile, knowing he did not believe it.

"Do not listen to anything she says. Besides, when did you ever?" Mercy whispered as she rubbed a comforting circle between her twin's shoulder blades.

"Mercy is correct," said Atticus, his pain on Felicity's behalf evident in his melancholy expression. "The viscountess no longer has influence on who you are and who you shall become."

Aware of the footsteps approaching behind them, Felicity only nodded her thanks to both her sister and her husband and turned to face the rest of their group. She was grateful Atticus knew to leave the subject on vague terms.

They had only just begun to tend the growing affection between them. They could not speak practically yet of children and childrearing. The mere thought still gripped Felicity in that familiar terror and apprehension, though its power was lessened the more she imagined Atticus sharing the role with her.

As if reading her mind, Atticus held up both hands with an expectant smile. Algernon replied first, nearly throwing Felicity off-balance with his eagerness to join his uncle, tiny fists reaching and grasping.

"There we are." Atticus laughed as the amiable boy danced in his arms.

Felicity's heart softened. Cool, fresh air flooded her lungs. It felt so right to see Atticus listening intently to his nephew's babbles as he swayed slowly from side to side. She nearly forgot everything that had just happened.

"He will make an excellent father, and you a loving mother,"

Mercy whispered into Felicity's ear, taking her hand and holding tightly when she felt her twin's uncomfortable squirm.

"You may not wish to hear it yet with all the other changes you are still accepting, but do not let our mother taint the happiness you now have and will have in the future if you remain open to it," she finished firmly without removing her earnest gaze from Felicity. "I cannot tell you how much joy it has brought me to see the transformation in you after such despair at the start."

Felicity squeezed her sister's hand in unspoken gratitude. "But what if she is right after all, just as she said?" Felicity mumbled with a shaky exhale.

Never had she encountered so many occasions to inspire such self-doubt and confusion within herself. She loathed the feeling. Why could she not allow herself to enjoy this new path and leave behind her old ideas and pains?

"How lovely it was to meet your family, Felicity!" said Arabella with exaggerated cheer as she came to stand beside her brother. "And most especially you, Miss—"

"Miss Reeve!"

The reunited group turned to find a footman scurrying toward them, his coat flapping in the wind. "Miss Reeve, her ladyship requests that you rejoin them immediately."

"It was my pleasure," Mercy answered quickly, offering her curtseys. "And it is an even greater pleasure to know that my beloved sister is so well cared for by her new family."

Mrs. Wheadon turned her fond smile to her daughter-in-law. "The pleasure has been entirely ours! Never have I met with such an articulately and enthusiastically expressed opinion. She has brought such excitement to our home that I must admit to feeling moments of guilt for stealing her from yours."

"Until next time, sister," Felicity said as she pulled Mercy into an embrace that both conveyed her sincerest appreciation and obscured the fierce blush that erupted across her face.

"You have nothing to fear, truly," was Mercy's only reply before quickly bidding her farewells and hurrying after the footman.

From somewhere behind them, quiet sniffles devolved into pitiful sobs. They whirled around to find Algernon tucked under his concerned uncle's chin.

"Poor little darling, whatever is the matter?" Arabella stepped closer to the pair and brushed her son's dark hair away from his forehead.

Algernon's red eyes landed upon Felicity. "Ahhh!" he cried with glee, sitting up and clumsily clapping.

Felicity started when she felt Mrs. Wheadon's kind, dainty hand upon her back. "Look at that! Algernon is completely taken with you, Felicity. He must have mistaken Miss Reeve for his aunt and clearly did not approve of her departure."

A gasp of realization rippled through the group and they began doting on Algernon with increased adoration, if such a thing were possible. It had become increasingly clear in this short time since the Hollingtons' arrival that the love surrounding this child would only grow as he did. The same would be true of Lydia and Sebastian's little one. At least, despite her own inner turmoil, Felicity could smile at that.

After attempting to return the young master to his pram and being met with vehement refusal, their party continued about the festival. Algernon remained happily perched in Atticus's arms. Walking in the back, Felicity chuckled to herself as she watched the boy repeatedly grasp at anything that came within reach while the uncle swept him away, whispering words of caution.

"He is quite devoted, is he not?" came Mrs. Wheadon's light voice from Felicity's left.

Felicity looked from her mother-in-law to her husband, who was now frantically attempting to pry a wooden lion figurine out of Algernon's mouth. "Indeed he is," she agreed with a fond sigh as she offered her arm.

The other woman accepted. They settled into an easy pace that fell a little behind the others. For several moments, the only sound that passed between the two Mrs. Wheadons was the soft click of their low heels on the street.

"Felicity…"

"Yes, madam?"

Watching the shorter woman from beneath her bonnet, Felicity's brows furrowed. She had never seen sweet, gregarious Mrs. Wheadon look so hesitant, her mouth unable to settle into a smile or frown. Had an alarm bell not begun sounding in the back of Felicity's mind, she might have laughed at the resemblance she was only just now witnessing between mother and son.

"I know, though we now share a name and a home—and love for that handsome young man there…" She paused and nodded toward Atticus. Her hesitation gave way to a loving smile that Felicity's heart mirrored as they watched him diligently brush Algernon's wayward hair out of his face.

"What I mean to say is," Mrs. Wheadon continued, "only time will strengthen our understanding of one another and foster a deeper familial closeness between us, but I hope, if it is not terribly impertinent, that you might begin to call me 'Mother.' And Mr. Wheadon would be honored should you choose to call him 'Father.' Only if it suits you, my dear. Neither of us would dream of forcing any discomfort upon you—"

Felicity interrupted, fighting another giggle. "I would be delighted…Mother." Apparently, Atticus and Mrs. Wheadon shared more than one surprising trait. She reached over to pat Mrs. Wheadon's hand where it rested atop hers.

Her new mother's bottom lip trembled in a pout. "I must say, I have recently discovered that my creative skills are more deficient than I thought. In all the times I imagined our boy's future wife in my prayers, I never imagined a lady as perfect as you."

Felicity's eyes widened, her heart swelling with an unexpected emotion—a strange mixture of her natural pride, genuine gratitude for Mrs. Wheadon's kind words, and, strangest of all…guilt. She had not quite become accustomed to the flowery compliments Atticus's parents lavished upon anyone and anything. Yet this was different. Each word had been chosen with care and infused with the utmost sincerity.

"Th-Thank you, but that is entirely too generous. I am *far* from perfect," Felicity answered under her breath.

Mrs. Wheadon gave a knowing chuckle. "We are all far from perfect, child. We are too complex with our individual histories layered upon natural temperaments. On the note of individual histories, if I may risk impertinence once more..."

"There are no impertinences with me," Felicity offered. Her shoulders went rigid with apprehension.

"I do not pretend to have full knowledge of your life before you became part of ours, other than the little Atticus has shared and, well, that business..."

Felicity fixed her gaze straight ahead at the group of musicians on the corner. She would not lower her head to her mother ever again, even in conversation with another.

"Yes, the business of my family. It is not entirely pleasant, as you seem to have surmised," Felicity added, giving Mrs. Wheadon a reassuring smile.

"All families have their unique challenges...some more than others," the older woman admitted in a glum tone. "But I do hope you remember that the challenges that plagued one generation need not be inherited by the next. I assure you with all my heart that I have seen nothing but the strongest of indications of the loving, caring mother you will soon become, because I have seen the depth of your love for Atticus. You are everything he needs and exactly what he deserves."

Felicity's stomach twisted. It was the very thing she longed to hear. It terrified her all the same. Her eyes drifted away from the musicians, blissfully unaware that their happy songs clashed with her gloom, to her husband.

As if witnessing a scene from some distant future, Felicity watched as Atticus laughed along with the baby held securely in his strong arms. From this angle, she could not discern Algernon's features, only the shining, dark hair that matched his uncle's.

Everything inside Felicity longed to believe Mrs. Wheadon's endorsement. To believe in herself. It should not have been difficult. When had Felicity ever struggled to believe in herself or encountered a challenge she did not overcome?

But she could not deny the fear that had been building inside her since she had been forced to turn her mind to matters of motherhood with Lydia's news.

What if Mrs. Wheadon was wrong? What if Felicity failed? What if she truly was not meant for this life?

She would be dooming an innocent child to the same pain she had suffered while simultaneously depriving Atticus of the partner he had always deserved.

That reality sat as heavy as a brick wall on Felicity's chest, on the fragile happiness she had finally dared let herself feel, a reminder of the truths increasingly demanding her attention. The truths that would not remain in the dark for much longer.

CHAPTER FOURTEEN

ATTICUS WATCHED FROM the drawing room window as Felicity marched across the lawn toward the treeline and Huxley Manor beyond for her daily visit with Mercy, a ritual never to be disturbed. He chuckled when he saw her pull her mustard shawl tighter about her, his breath leaving a fog on the glass.

Unsurprisingly, Atticus's wife had refused his offer of the carriage so she might travel in warmth for the short ride. She was such a creature of fresh air, he suspected she would continue to refuse until the heavier snows began. Algernon had loved that. He'd always had someone to take him out of doors when his small hands reached for the windows. In fact, the boy had immediately taken to Felicity and revealed an endearingly tender and exceedingly caring side to Atticus's wife that he had not yet witnessed.

Longing struck Atticus's heart at the thought of his dear sister, brother-in-law, and nephew. A week had passed far more quickly than he had thought possible, and their departure, only two days past, would still ache until he received word of their safe return to Derbyshire and assurances of an enjoyable visit.

"Ah, Atticus, I have been dispatched to dispatch you."

Atticus jumped, his forehead thumping against the thick glass. Grimacing and rubbing the sore spot, he turned to Papa in the doorway. "By whom and to where?"

"By your mother, to the music room," the older man answered with an amused smile. "Most likely something about tonight's grand dinner."

Atticus's stomach sprang into knots once more. Only Felicity's presence, or thoughts of her, had been keeping Atticus from melting into a puddle of anxiety at the prospect.

Did it have to be so soon after a social visit? As much as Atticus loved his younger sister and her darling family, he had been looking forward to a period of respite in the privacy of his library, with only his wife for company. But, with such sociable parents, they had felt the loss of Arabella, Samuel, and Algernon quite keenly and sought to fill it as quickly as possible.

"All will be well, son," Papa offered quietly as Atticus joined him at the drawing room door. He clapped a hand on the younger man's shoulder and squeezed.

Atticus replied with a smile of appreciation. Though they were as different as parent and child could be in many ways, both Papa and Mama had always treated Atticus's nerves with sympathy.

Up one more flight of stairs, Atticus heard the skilled rendition of some familiar piece whose name always escaped him drifting down the hall. It ceased the moment he stepped foot into the music room.

"Atticus! Thank heavens your papa did not have to search for you through that labyrinth of a library." Mama laughed as she rose from the bench and ushered Atticus to the pair of chairs in the corner.

"He mentioned you wished to discuss the dinner?" Atticus asked as he took his seat.

"In truth, I wished to ask your lovely wife's opinion since she is acting as hostess alongside me, but since Lambert informed me that she has just departed, I thought I would see if you might know."

"K-Know what?" Atticus's heart rate gained speed. He was not fond of being asked to consult on such important matters. He especially did not wish to give an incorrect impression of Felicity's desires for her very first officially hosted event.

Sensing Atticus's mounting anxiety, Mama reached across the small table and took his hand. "It is only a minor dilemma, I assure you. We chose light orange and yellow for the napkins, an autumnal theme, but I have just been informed by the house-keeper that several of the orange napkins have suffered some unfortunate discoloration. Do you think Felicity would prefer cream to replace them or the red?"

"Red."

Mama's brows arched up, a pleased smile spreading across her face. "You had that answer quite at the ready."

"Mama," Atticus grumbled, slumping down into his chair a little further.

"Oh, can you blame me? I am simply happy to see my son so in love!" she cried, waving away his youthful embarrassment. "But you are certain red would be Felicity's choice? Not that she would mind terribly either way, I am sure. She has been so agreeable and accepting of all my advice. Still, since it is her very first event as a married woman, I should like her to have everything as near to perfection as possible."

The heat in Atticus's face subsided. He did love to hear his mother speak so fondly of his wife and to know that they shared their duties as two generations of Mrs. Wheadon amicably. Of course, Atticus had also noticed the ladies' growing closeness since Mama's return in no small part thanks to Felicity's increasingly frequent reports of her adoration for her mother-in-law.

"I am certain," he answered, his normally tremulous voice confident. "Felicity would prefer the bolder color—perhaps most especially *because* it is her first event. She is always finding such fascinating ways to announce herself to the world, unafraid."

"She is a wonderfully bold young lady, indeed," Mama agreed with a knowing nod. "Just what you needed."

Atticus could not help his soft smile. He unfocused his gaze. Everything faded away but Felicity. He truly must have looked a fool in love. For possibly the first time in his life, Atticus did not care. To display his feelings for Felicity on his face was no shameful thing.

"You are absolutely correct, Mama. Even now, as I feel the nerves plaguing my mind ahead of tonight's event, they are markedly lessened. I only need think of my wife to remember that all will be well. If, by some terrible chance, the dinner is a complete disaster and our guests leave in disgust, never to return, I know Felicity will still be there. She will always be there."

Glancing up, Atticus noticed a mist in Mama's eyes as she pressed a hand over her mouth. "Precisely, dear boy. You have the measure of marriage now. Goodness, how grown you have become! You and Arabella both. I am living every mother's greatest dream."

A dream Atticus knew Mama had had good reason to doubt when it came to her son. Indeed, Atticus had not always made that burden easy for his parents to bear with his continual avoidance or dismissal of the topic of matrimony. He reached across the small table between them and engulfed Mama's hand in his, holding tight.

"Thank you—you and Papa—for living such a fine example for us. I suppose you were right, that there truly is someone for each person, no matter how…unique."

"Dear Atticus." The woman sighed, squeezing back. "As your mama, who has thought you perfection since the moment I knew I carried you, please do not take offense if I suggest that no one views you as you do yourself. You are indeed unique in many ways, but not in the ways you fear. Felicity certainly seems to believe so."

To Atticus's immense surprise, her expression darkened. "Mama?"

Starting, Mama quickly smoothed her features, but they did not quite return to her usual cheer. "Forgive me. It is just that I still occasionally recall that day at the festival… I did not hear all, but I certainly heard and saw enough. And weighing my own observations with the bits you have revealed… Well, I must say it does not paint a very pleasant picture of Felicity's youth."

"Certainly a very different picture than our family's," Atticus agreed, lowering his head.

Now that Felicity had given Atticus the story of her life's events and relations as well as the feelings they produced in minute detail, his pity for his cherished wife had only increased. To know the extent of her neglect—particularly cold even for the less-than-affectionate standards of the *ton*'s parents—and the deep scars it had left threatened to break Atticus's heart anew every time he thought of it.

"I confess I stole an opportunity to speak with Felicity about the matter that day while you all were occupied with Algernon and the festivities."

Atticus's head lifted sharply. "Did you? She was not distressed?"

Mama shook her head. "No, not distressed. But it was evident that her former situation still pains her. Understandably, of course, after enduring it for so long without any hope of change."

"She is still coming to accept that there is no shame in admitting she has been wounded. It will be a slow journey, but a worthwhile one. I can hardly fathom what it would do to me to only see you and Papa one month out of the entire year before coming out into Society."

"A terrible shame," Mama agreed, each word heavy with sympathy. Even her gray-tinged curls seemed weighed down as she hung her head. "And I am afraid it has caused her to doubt her own capability…"

"For what?"

"Well, with such an example for a mother, can you blame the poor dear for being concerned for her own future as a mother? I sensed that she still had her misgivings, but she was so lovely with Algernon.

"In truth, every parent who means to do the job credibly with some degree of personal involvement frets over their suitability for such a monumental task. What Felicity feels—what I suspect you both feel—is quite normal, I assure you. Though perhaps you both have your own reasons for feeling it more keenly than others might."

Atticus's eyes widened. "Y-You surmised all that, did you?"

A rare burst of giggles, completely unrestrained by manners, spilled from Mama, her narrow shoulders shaking. After his initial moment of surprise, Atticus joined with his own sheepish chuckle.

She gasped between renewed fits of laughter. "My love, I am your mother. I always know. And someday—sooner than you think, for the days do begin to fly—you will know, too."

Despite the much-needed levity, guilt still squeezed Atticus's chest. His mother did not *always* know. Not everything. His parents still remained ignorant of his marriage's origins. There was some relief in knowing that, now that he and Felicity had transformed their circumstances into a love match, his parents need never know the truth.

"But, Mama," Atticus started, his quiet voice growing stronger with each word, "I have been so long convinced that I am not meant for a shared life. Not with anyone who breathes air instead of ink.

"And, naturally, now that I have found someone I cherish and must truly contend with desires I have never allowed myself to desire…a kindred soul, little ones with golden hair… my anxieties have increased a hundred—no, a thousandfold. Something terrible could happen at any moment. How could I possibly bear it, to lose one so dear or to leave them behind—"

"Atticus." Mama raised her voice over his, holding up a hand for silence.

He paused and inhaled. The rush of air into his lungs nearly sent him into a dizzy spell. He had not realized he'd expelled all of that in one breath.

"I know you believe us to be of extremely different temperaments," she continued with a fond, understanding smile, "but do not be fooled. Again, we may not experience with the same depth, but such worrisome thoughts have passed through my mind and your father's. It is natural to fret over the well-being of one's family. Allowing that worry to consume you will only rob you of the precious happiness you should be sharing with the ones you love while they are here."

"But if we are both terrified—"

"That means you both understand the responsibility, and that is hardly a flaw. If I may offer one more piece of advice?"

Atticus rolled his shoulders, encouraging his muscles to relax. "Of course, Mama."

Her other hand came to rest atop Atticus's.

"Speak to your wife. I know you may have shared shades of your feelings, but do not be afraid to deepen them. I suspect it will bring Felicity as much relief as it does you. Do you see how much you have already affected each other? You would not have spoken so freely and bravely with me about such intimate matters before our arrival in Bainbridge. In the same way you strengthen each other's shortcomings in your marriage, so to it shall be in your nursery. And for any other challenges you face, for that matter."

"We must rely upon one another," Atticus added under his breath.

"You *do* have the measure of marriage, it seems." Mama chuckled, patting his hand. "Why don't you ready yourself for dinner? Goodness, and to think we began with napkin colors!"

"Thank you, Mama," Atticus said as he rose. He leaned down and placed a light kiss upon her cap.

As he quit the music room and wound through Setherwell to his quarters, a rare spark of courage burned deep in his chest. Perhaps he could finally allow himself to accept Mama's words.

He could not have managed it alone. But anything was possible with Felicity by his side, loving and accepting him just as he did her. Though they had yet to say as much aloud, perhaps the time had come.

Atticus could feel it in every flutter of his heart, in every weightless step. Beyond all his wildest dreams, he had fallen headfirst into love. It was a miracle not to be wasted.

Together, he and Felicity would face their fears, heal their wounds, and create a new future. It was all possible, but only if she was there. Atticus could wait no longer. For once, the exhilaration of risk raced through him. For once, he believed he had found something in which he could not fail.

CHAPTER FIFTEEN

A VERY DIFFERENT type of apprehension plagued Atticus as he paced up and down the library shelves, illuminated by candlelight and a faint glow from the fireplace. The precise location where their lives had changed forever. For the better.

He had been waiting for Felicity since he had received word of her return from Huxley, but she had gone straight upstairs to change. Several minutes ago, a maid had appeared in the doorway to inform Atticus that Felicity had torn the hem of her gown and required another change.

Atticus's eyes darted to the clock on the marble mantle. The hope with which he had strode into the library after his conversation with Mama was all but extinguished. Their neighbors would be arriving soon—far too soon for all he longed to say and all he longed to hear in return.

"Please forgive my tardiness!" Felicity's bright voice called from somewhere behind Atticus.

"Felicity." Atticus held out a hand toward his wife, resplendent in a blue, silk gown with intricate, silver beading, cheeks flushed with her haste.

She took his hand and wove their fingers together. He felt the stiffness ease from Felicity as they inhaled in unison. The rhythms of their very beings fell into place.

Atticus's hopes of walking into the drawing room arm in arm and confident in the next chapter of their journey may have been dashed, yet his newfound confidence remained. When Felicity gazed up at him with that profound certainty that Atticus recognized in his own soul, he knew.

He knew that once he laid his naked heart at Felicity's feet—shedding every layer of worry, self-doubt, guilt, past circumstances—he would succeed.

Tilting her head to one side, diamond tiara shimmering in the warm flickers of candlelight, Felicity grinned. A strange sense of inevitability overcame Atticus. It almost felt as if they had said it all in that single look. Still, the words lingering on the tip of his tongue would require release later. After dinner, when their world became quiet and still once more, just the two of them.

"Are you ready?" Felicity whispered after another long, silent breath.

Atticus grinned back. "I am."

He knew the nerves would return when the multitude of people began spilling into his home, eager for hours of entertainment. Threading Felicity's arm through his, Atticus knew he was ready to endure them.

Outside the drawing room doors, Atticus paused. He turned to Felicity and brought one hand to her face, tracing the soft planes of her cheek to her jaw. A muscle in Felicity's neck twitched. Her eyes lowered to Atticus's mouth.

"You make this so much easier than I ever thought possible," he whispered against her temple. Her hair tickled the tip of his nose and Atticus inhaled her scent.

"As do you, in so many ways," she replied, warm breath caressing Atticus's skin.

"Well now, there you are!" Papa's voice boomed from down the hall, followed by an echoing clap.

The young pair jumped apart, still not quite used to their privilege of physical proximity as a married couple. Atticus offered a prayer of gratitude for the shadows in the hall as embarrassment scorched his face.

"I swear, your mama has sent me all over this house in search of you today." The older man laughed as he approached. "Now when I go in search of you again, I find you precisely where you are meant to be."

Papa fixed them with a proud gaze as he settled one hand on Atticus's shoulder and the other on Felicity's. Despite his mortification at being interrupted during a moment of spontaneous affection, Atticus could not help a small smile. Papa did not realize how correct he was. Or perhaps he did, judging by the glint in his amused eyes.

"You both look dazzling," he continued. "Shall we? Your mother is already inside, flying about to ensure the finishing touches are still finished."

Atticus and Felicity exchanged glances and nodded.

The four Wheadons only had a few minutes to gather themselves before the first guests, the Abbott and Gardiner families, were announced. The Harrowsmiths and Daileys followed shortly thereafter, and then several more couples and families from Bainbridge, including the Reeves.

As Atticus had predicted, his usual worries continued to escalate as more and more people arrived. Enveloped as he was in the haze of falling in love, where time held no relevance, this cacophony of strange voices surrounding him was a harsh reminder that Atticus had only lived among them for three months.

He had only known Felicity for three months. Atticus, the one who never dared rush a decision, even one as inconsequential as which cravat to wear at dinner, had found love and married in a matter of weeks. It sounded more like a fairy tale Atticus might read on a rainy summer night than his own life.

Gliding about the room, effortlessly conversing and smiling abundantly, Atticus's wife looked every bit the enchanting princess he pictured in his mind's eye when he read those magical stories.

Somehow, he had unintentionally chosen the best corner from which to observe Felicity's natural talents as hostess. Much like Mama, she visited every cluster of guests for several minutes each, lending her ear and wearing an inviting smile. Atticus was only too happy to watch her glow under the candelabras and bask in the compliments of her neighbors from his spot, quiet and tucked away.

"Mr. Wheadon!"

The familiar, airy voice of Miss Clara Gardiner sounded to Atticus's right. He leaned forward and peered around the large vase blocking his peripheral vision. The young lady did the same, curls springing delightfully.

"I do hope we are not overwhelming you. Or boring you! Heavens, I cannot think which would be more dreadful." She laughed as she joined Atticus in his corner.

"Neither, Miss Clara, I assure you," Atticus said with a chuckle of his own. "I trust the evening is meeting your expectations thus far?"

Aside from the amiable Mr. Harrowsmith, the sweet, good-natured Gardiner sisters had quickly become Atticus's favorites of his new Bainbridge friends. Miss Clara wrinkled her nose and shook her head.

"Mr. Wheadon, you are too humble! The evening has already exceeded my every expectation tremendously. I applaud you all!"

Atticus waved a hand, his eyes once again finding Felicity in the shifting crowd by the fireplace, this time with the elder Mrs. Harrowsmith and her younger counterpart.

"Thank you, but you direct your applause at the incorrect party. I hardly lifted a hand compared to my parents and Felicity. It would appear they are all great lovers of the art of hosting, from planning to execution."

Miss Clara looked in the direction of Atticus's gaze. "She always thought she would hate it," she replied under her breath. "Of course, she suspected she'd be amidst strangers if she ever married—and then she'd be forced to spend all her time and energy preparing these grand events for people she hardly knows or cares for, being paraded about like a prized mare. Our Felicity does have quite a way with words when she has a mind for it," she finished, hiding her grin behind a silken hand.

"Indeed she does," Atticus agreed. "I am glad she appears not to feel as though she is a hostess against her will."

"Not at all! In fact, she appears to be enjoying herself a great deal. She is a willing and proud participant because she is proud of her new home and family."

Warmth released the tension in Atticus's muscles. Having Felicity's happiness confirmed by his parents, who possessed a natural bias toward him, was one thing. Having it confirmed by those who had known Felicity longest, who knew her best, was another thing entirely.

"I am immensely pleased to hear you say so," Atticus replied, lowering his head in a grateful bow. "I plan to ensure she continues to enjoy herself a great deal every day."

The whimsical young lady's hands flew to her face, cupping her round cheeks as she let out a satisfied sigh.

"I know you will, sir. It is written, after all. Just like Lydia and Sebastian, a foretold happy ending. They have been the dearest friends their entire lives, yet they only found their way to each other with Lady Swan's help. Of course there can be no doubt of their eternal contentment, or yours and Felicity's."

Lady Swan.

A memory buried in the back of Atticus's mind surged forward. "P-Pardon?"

Miss Clara's eyes widened, her breath quickening.

"Oh, just Lydia and Sebastian, you see," she hurried, pointing in the direction of the younger Mrs. Harrowsmith. "Being only a month apart in age and raised on adjoining properties, they have shared a particular closeness since their earliest days, even closer than the rest of our little circle."

Atticus's polite smile tightened. "Ah, I do recall now. But...you mentioned a Lady Swan?"

"I-Indeed? Well, you see, it is a little difficult to define precisely because, well, we do not know who she is."

The deep well of panic that had always lived inside Atticus, that had been kept at bay by this blissful, waking dream, threatened to shoot up like a fountain and drown him in his old fears.

"And how might Lady Swan be involved in—"

"Dinner is served!"

The butler's bellow sliced through idle conversation. In a blink, Miss Clara had returned to her older sister's side halfway across the drawing room, blending in with the crush of guests as they funneled toward the dining room doors.

Atticus forced himself to engage in the motions throughout the remainder of the evening. Had his mental state not suffered such an unexpected shock, he might have thought it a little pitiful how quickly he resumed that feeling of being half in the room and half in the dungeon of his own mind.

As always, he survived by employing his favorite technique of staying as much out of the way as possible and allowing whoever came within his vicinity to focus the conversation on themselves, leaving him to nod and hum along at regular intervals. All the while, Miss Clara's words echoed in his mind—the name of Lady Swan most of all.

"Congratulations to you both on a spectacular evening!" Mama cheered as the drawing room door closed behind the last guest. She flew to Atticus and Felicity and threw her arms around them.

"I suspect our fellow hosts are in need of rest. I know I certainly am," Papa added with a muffled yawn, one hand rubbing his straining vest.

The older couple bid goodnight to the younger and quit the drawing room, arm in arm with Mrs. Wheadon's head resting against Mr. Wheadon's shoulder. Atticus did not know how he could have grown up with the truest example of love before his eyes and still been so terrified of it.

"Shall we?" Felicity asked just before the door. She looked over her shoulder at Atticus, one brow raised expectantly.

No, staring at his wife from across the room, Atticus knew how. Because no matter how much closer he thought he came to understanding and accepting love, he still found himself facing a question whose answer could very well crush him.

"Atticus?"

Beautiful Felicity turned away from the door and took several steps toward him. There was that dauntless, curious glint in her dark eyes. Her pink lips parted, on the verge of another question.

"Who is Lady Swan?"

The question hung in the air between them. Only the faint ticking of the grandfather clock on the opposite wall punctuated the silence. Atticus lost count of the seconds. They both stood rooted to their positions.

Eventually, Felicity deflated, her rigid shoulders dropping. But her head did not hang. Her eyes remained fixed on Atticus, resolved.

"I do not know. None of us do. Lydia was the first to receive a letter from her last Season. It contained hints guiding Lydia toward her perfect match, with an uncanny personal knowledge of them both. And, well, you have seen the result of her work."

The words trickled out haltingly. The ache of uncertainty that had gripped Atticus's chest all evening squeezed tighter. This was not like his Felicity. He could see it in her restless fingers worrying away at the silk sash around her waist. Atticus could read her behaviors so well in such little time, yet he had clearly missed a significant indicator that something was indeed quite wrong...and had been wrong for longer than he'd realized.

"And Lady Swan is a false name?"

"It would appear so. There were a few initial theories and attempts to unmask her. But, in truth, we all became preoccupied with solving the mystery of whom Lydia was being guided toward, and of course the drama of our own experiences of the Season. Thus, Lady Swan's true identity remains unknown."

"You received a letter. Directing you toward me."

A statement, not a question. The pieces of a much larger

puzzle that had begun the moment he'd stepped foot in Bainbridge fell into place.

Felicity's gaze answered the painful truth. She nodded once.

As the pieces fell into place, Atticus's heart fell apart. The false pretenses had not begun with their marriage. They had begun before Atticus had even arrived. His blood boiled in his veins with mortification and misery as he stared back at the woman he loved so desperately. The woman he needed.

"You are here because of a letter," Atticus whispered.

His mind spun, parsing every precious memory for the glimpses of truth Atticus had been too daft to notice. Perhaps he had not wanted to notice them. The feeling of being seen and understood, of laying bare his entire vulnerable being with another, free of judgment, had been too intoxicating. He had not appreciated how impactful that liberation had been to his spirit until this moment.

Worse still, he had thought the feeling had been reciprocated. Despite the remarkable progress their unlikely marriage had made, despite the intimacy Atticus had thought they had begun to foster, his wife had not been able to bring herself to reveal this letter. In fact, she did not appear to have had any intention of ever revealing it. He yet again found himself unbalanced, unsure of his place in the world—of his place in Felicity's world.

Her eyes fell to the ground. "It began that way…"

"And that is why you were watching me the day we arrived—because you were curious. That is why you hid in the gardens on the day of the welcome luncheon—because you were determined not to marry, to avoid me. That is why…you followed me into the library… because…"

Atticus dragged the words out, each one scraping against his raw throat. His heart hammered in a way he had never experienced before. How could he have been ignorant of such a detail for so long? What other information about his wife and their relationship might remain hidden from him? "It began that way…" she repeated slowly.

"Felicity, I..." Atticus attempted a shuddering inhale.

"Yes?" Even with her head lowered, her hands twisting around each other, she still encouraged him.

"Why did you not tell me sooner? I thought we'd shared everything..."

Felicity's expression contorted and she turned her face away. "Because I did not *want* Lady Swan's letter. I never wanted one. But she disregarded my very vocal aspirations to spinsterhood.

"How was I to explain that to a stranger? Especially after the night of the ball and finding myself so unexpectedly and permanently attached to you, I felt even less at liberty to reveal Lady Swan's role. The situation was already so unwelcome to us both that I could not bear to make it any more complex. And now here I stand..."

Her voice trailed away into the low crackle of firelight. She still did not meet Atticus's eye. That was the most worrisome indicator of all.

How could he have been so blind? How could he have been so wrong? Even Mama was wrong.

Just hours ago, Atticus had been armed with all the confidence he had ever managed to muster in his life to throw off his fears and give his whole heart to his wife. And now...

"And now here you stand...married to me because of an anonymous matchmaker's letter."

In a strange reversal of their natures, Felicity fell silent while Atticus's pain and shame spurred him on.

"I thought you fell in love with me...because of me. I thought someone had seen me just as I am and accepted it, wanted it. Without Lady Swan, you would never have looked in my direction. Instead, I became an obstacle to your true desire because you were given reason to take notice of me."

Felicity's perfect lips trembled. Even from halfway across the room, for neither of them dared move an inch closer with this wall of the unsaid between them, Atticus could see the glisten in her eyes.

"I thought we trusted each other. I thought we had achieved full openness and honesty between each other. I thought I had finally solved the mystery of coming to truly understand another soul. And now I find that I am far more naive than I feared."

His soul crumbled to see her distress, knowing he was the cause, while his mind hissed in that deepest, darkest corner that after this uncomfortable business, in some strange way, Felicity would be free. If she did not truly love Atticus as he had come to believe, heartache would be no imprisonment for her.

For the only heart broken, it would be a lifelong punishment. This was for the best, Atticus reasoned to himself. Better his heart than hers, certainly. Felicity had endured more than enough already. But could Atticus endure it?

There was no other choice. He had outrun even himself.

"Please do not think to spare me. I seek honesty only, no secrets." Atticus paused and braced himself. Terrified or not, he must know. "If the discovery had not been forced, did you ever plan to tell me about Lady Swan?"

CHAPTER SIXTEEN

"I AM SORRY." The words slipped from Felicity's mouth, almost slurred. She saw, heard, felt everything in slow motion. The very edges of the drawing room blurred.

Was this truly happening? She hardly realized what she was saying. But she must. She could never, ever see such a tortured expression on Atticus's face again or be the cause of it. This had gone well out of hand. She had been caught completely out of her depth and done something terrible as a result. She had broken Atticus's trust.

"I am so, so sorry."

Her husband took a step back. Much farther and he would go right through the wall. Atticus never did take much heed of his surroundings, a trait that had brought Felicity much amusement over the past few months. She wished she had known then that those would be some of the last times amusement or joy would color her life.

"I-Is there anything else I should know?" he pressed without any real urgency.

Her sweet Atticus had become so brave, so assured in himself. So much so that he had not removed his gaze from her until now. He already did not trust whatever reply she would make.

"No, I promise," Felicity insisted, almost breathless. Her heart twisted when he did not look at her. "Atticus, you must know I care for you more deeply than words can express."

Felicity could not bring herself to hate the trembling in her tone. It had been astoundingly foolish to think it could have ended any differently. Not for someone like her.

Now, thanks to her own stubbornness, she had trapped Atticus into a marriage founded on dishonesty, robbing him of the life he deserved with someone who would no doubt have handled his precious heart with more care.

What else had Felicity expected? She was never meant to be the tender, selfless partner whom Atticus needed. Her nature was that of a storm and always would be—reckless and unwelcome.

Atticus had finally seen the truth of it. How could he not? Felicity's own incurable flaws blinded her, forcing her to blink back tears. She had brought this upon herself and doomed an innocent man in the process.

It was unforgivable. The gradual resignation in her husband's handsome face told her as much.

"I would have understood," he said under his breath, wounded gaze on the floor. "At least, I think I would have. I suppose we shall never know now."

Another crescendo of deafening silence filled the chasm between Felicity and Atticus. She did not know how long they stood in total stillness. The sensation spread through her body like a rash, urging her to jump, scream, tear off and shatter the jewels constricting her throat—to run far away, to run forever. To run straight into the safety of her familiar fears.

Stillness would never be the same for her. Not like it was when Atticus stood beside her. Felicity would never find peace again, so what would be the harm in running?

"Perhaps this was a mistake."

Atticus flinched. Felicity felt the air squeeze out of her lungs. Still, his focus remained anywhere but on her. How desperately she longed to look into his lovely eyes yet could not bear to see the pain of her betrayal in them.

Her husband had put his full, fragile trust in Felicity. She, in turn, though not intentionally, had made a fool of him. Indeed,

Atticus should have known much, much sooner. He was, after all, the bearer of equal consequence in Lady Swan's scheme—and the bearer of unfair burden in this marriage that was entirely Felicity's fault.

The faults did not end there. Of course, Felicity's pride had prevented her from admitting that she may not have been capable of this miraculous change, the change that had allowed her to open her heart to Atticus, without another's assistance.

"A mistake?" Atticus echoed.

"All of this," Felicity continued quickly before she could lose her nerve. She pleaded to the guarded air surrounding her husband as he half-turned away from her, brows furrowing. "From the very beginning, I have made so many mistakes. I cannot tell you how sorry I am that you are paying the price for them as well. I never should have encouraged either of us to think I deserved your faith and...love."

Love. The word seized Felicity's chest in a cruel grip. Neither of them had actually said it aloud to each other yet. She hated that she had lost her opportunity to hear him offer it to her with warmth, with tenderness. Then again, she could not be sure if such a memory would bring her more comfort or remorse in the lonely days to come.

"What would you have me do?"

"Do?" Felicity repeated dumbly. There was nothing more either of them *could* do. They had known that since the moment Felicity had stepped into the library, what felt like a lifetime ago now.

Atticus's hands clenched and unclenched at his sides. A nervous habit Felicity had slowly begun to unwind by placing her hand in his when she'd noticed it.

Did he long to reach for her now? Felicity shook her head, a tear falling loose. She brushed it away with her knuckles. It was far more likely that he despised her than longed for her.

She could hardly blame him. She despised herself. Felicity's battered, quaking heart whispered a reminder that she was doing what was best, even if neither of them felt it yet.

"H-How do you wish to proceed? A return to the early days?"

Felicity squeezed her eyes shut. She hated to hear that tremble in his voice, not anxiety but pain.

How could they ever hope to overcome this hurdle? How could Atticus ever believe anything Felicity said of her feelings now? "Y-Yes, I think that would be wise."

Each word sliced her to her core. Felicity finally lowered her head. When had she ever cared for the wise course? She certainly did not feel wise at present. In fact, she was sure no greater fool had ever walked this Earth than she. Felicity was a complete and utter fool for thinking she could have a kind of happiness she had not known possible, a happiness where freedom was found in the safety of another's kind, patient soul.

"As you wish."

Those three syllables hammered the nails into the coffin. Felicity felt each one in the depths of her hollow stomach.

Before Felicity realized what was happening, Atticus's hesitant step forward became a rush toward her. No, not toward her. Past her. His eyes remained fixed on the floor, his strides giving him a wide berth around Felicity.

"Atticus, I am sorry," she blurted out as he came parallel to her.

He paused. His head remained lowered. His hands had stilled. "I know."

There was nothing more to be said. Atticus quit the drawing room. Felicity stood in the center for an untold amount of time, her head tilted back. She stared up at the artful swirls and swoops of the white moulding that crept across the ceiling to form an even bigger and more breathtaking pattern in the center. Strange that she had never thought to appreciate it until now.

The tears that had pooled in her eyes, bridled by sheer force of will, flowed freely down her cheeks and neck and into her hair. She had always hated that wet, pitiful feeling tears produced. For now, she had not the energy to care.

Somehow, despite cherishing every precious moment with Atticus as they'd occurred, Felicity found herself still wishing she had appreciated them more profoundly. Her eyes drifted closed. Then again, if she had realized then what would come to pass now, perhaps she would have never allowed it to develop further.

She never would have experienced this range of wondrous emotions and the fullness of contentment only found in true acceptance. She never would have experienced this all-encompassing sorrow that threw a harsh light upon her many deficiencies—not the least of which being the unjustness of the pity she felt for herself. Heavy muscles twitched, the last vestiges of her energy calling for release.

Innocent, unselfish, obliging Atticus had suffered the greatest. Because of Felicity.

What right did she have to flee from the drawing room, tears flying behind her, and slam her bedroom door behind her with a whimper? What right did she have to behave as though she were the wretched one when she could only imagine the agony in the room not two walls away from hers? She was no tragic heroine from one of Atticus's books. She was the antagonist.

Her back still pressed against her door, Felicity lowered her face into her hands. Her shoulders shook, every inch of her skin ablaze.

"What have you done?" Felicity groaned.

She did not know which of her innumerable missteps she addressed. Perhaps every one she had taken from the very moment she'd received Lady Swan's letter had been a misstep. All these months, Felicity had thought she had chosen a path of caution when she had really done the same as she always had from the very start: act without thinking to the vexation and detriment of everyone around her.

Peeling herself away from the door, Felicity dragged her aching body to the bed and fell face-first amongst her many plump pillows. She had just begun to burrow under the covers when a knock sounded.

"Madam, shall I ready you for bed?" called her lady's maid.

"Not now, Hammond," Felicity replied without lifting her face from the comfort of her pillows.

"Pardon?"

With a pained grumble, Felicity forced her head up. "Later, please, Hammond!"

"C-Certainly, madam. Are you quite well? Might I fetch you anything?"

"No, but I do thank you," Felicity answered with as much softness as she could muster. A moment of hesitation and Hammond's footsteps retreated down the hall.

"This is quite beyond human intervention, I am afraid," Felicity added under her breath as she pulled the blanket over her head.

The surrounding softness and darkness had helped to soothe Felicity's aching heart as a child. It had protected her from the pain inflicted by others, if only for a night of fitful sleep. Yet no matter how Felicity twisted or wrapped herself, the tears and grief continued, relentless.

Because she was the one who had inflicted this pain upon herself and upon an undeserving heart. Not Lady Swan. Not her own mother. No one had made Felicity's choices but Felicity.

From this fact she could not hide. No one else owned the blame but her.

CHAPTER SEVENTEEN

FELICITY DID NOT appear at breakfast the following morning. It should not have injured Atticus to see her empty chair as much as it did. His grip tightened around his fork.

What else had he expected? To wake up and go about his day in the hopes that last night had been a horrible dream populated by his few hours of rest? That fool's hope could never have lasted beyond breakfast.

Felicity was not here. They would never share a breakfast together again.

His heart plummeted yet again. Throwing his napkin onto the dining table, Atticus pushed himself to his feet, his appetite evaporated. Of the few sips and bites he'd forced upon himself, none of them had tasted right. It was all bland. Lifeless.

Just like that, Atticus's world had returned to gray. It had always been bound to. How could something as delicate as love grow upon such an illusory foundation? Yet his had, without his permission, without his realizing until it had been too late.

Atticus had unknowingly been playing his part, almost as if he were a character in a story, placed just so, to fulfill a role and not a living, breathing, breakable man.

He slumped forward and planted his palms on the solid-wood table. All this time, he had thought he was growing in strength and courage by allowing himself to open his heart. Instead, Atticus had only welcomed a type of pain he had never thought to prepare himself for: the pain of betrayal. And of how he had been embarrassingly naive.

He shook his head in a feeble attempt to cast away that nagging feeling in the pit of his stomach that perhaps he had too readily accepted his wounded pride's vehement insistence that he accept her withdrawal and do the same himself.

Still, this was precisely the dreadful ache that had always filled Atticus with terror, that he tried desperately to escape in novels...that he thought he'd finally broken free from with the help of his brilliant wife. She was brilliant indeed, yet would it have been fair to Atticus to look at Felicity in the course of their daily lives and wonder, in the faintest whisper in the furthest corner of his mind, if he might be caught unawares again?

Atticus had come to believe that Felicity was the one person who would always be honest with him. To realize that even she could withhold such a pivotal secret had been a shock Atticus had never imagined, not now.

Worse still, he had forced Felicity to do the one thing she had never wanted...even if she had seemed content eventually.

Despite his every good intention and effort, Atticus had become the cage she'd always feared. That much had been evident in her eyes last night.

"Dear Atticus, whatever is the matter?"

Mama's frantic cry disrupted the unceasing bombardment of Atticus's shameful thoughts. He straightened and turned to find both parents racing across the breakfast room. They snatched at his hands and face, feeling for an elevated temperature or a wound, showering a volley of worried questions upon Atticus's already fractured mind.

"Stop, please," he mumbled under his breath. His shoulders inched up around his ears as he tried to gain a modicum of distance.

"Goodness gracious, was it the fish from last night? Oh, I was so suspicious of that new preparation method Cook showed me!"

"Look here, let me have a look at you. So pale! Was the port too strong for your liking?"

"And where is Felici—"

"Stop, please!"

The breakfast room went still. Mama's and Papa's ministrations ceased. Atticus took a step back and turned away, clawing at his collar, desperate for air.

"Atticus...where is Felicity?" Mama repeated after a long, shocked silence.

"What's happened, son? Why don't you sit here and tell us?"

With exceeding gentleness, Papa approached and rested his fingertips upon Atticus's elbow, guiding him back to the long table laden with forlorn food and beverages. The footmen had brought in Felicity's usual hot chocolate before he had convinced himself that the events of last night had been very, very real.

With a deep sigh, he resumed his seat while his parents took the two closest on his left. Atticus was strangely appreciative of it. He was not yet ready to look up and see another face on his right but Felicity's.

"You have argued," Mama said.

Atticus nodded. If it could sound so simple, why could it not be just as simple to repair?

"All couples do, Atticus, even the supremely happy ones. Even us," she continued, her words laced with quiet optimism. Papa nodded his agreement.

"Not like this." Atticus sighed once more.

He hung his head, his dark fringe obscuring the sympathetic frowns on his parents' faces. He had no desire to see their expressions when he revealed his own deception.

"Whatever it is, surely, it is nothing the two of you cannot overcome with patience and time," Papa added.

"If we'd had a love match, perhaps."

Mama's stifled gasp broke Atticus's heart anew. "W-What do you mean to say?"

"It was a lie. A ruse." Atticus shrugged. He had never felt more defeated. "It was a mistake, apparently. She made it clear after dinner that she..."

"Atticus, you are not speaking sense. We have seen you together from the very start," Papa argued, his disbelief loud and clear.

"It would have been a grievous scandal. The night of the ball you hosted not long after our arrival... Felicity and I were caught unchaperoned in the library by Lady Eldmar."

"Atticus!" Mama jumped to her feet, her chair scraping against the wooden floor.

Atticus flinched and retreated further into his lanky frame. Though he still could not bring himself to look up, he heard the hum of Mama fanning herself under Papa's steady stream of whispered reassurances and attempts to return her to her seat.

"How could this happen?" she demanded, her voice cracking. "This is not to be borne! *Never* would I have thought *you* would be the one to compromise a young lady. And to lie to your mother and father, and for so long!"

"Dearest, please," Papa begged, finally managing to catch his wife's wrist as she paced back and forth in a flurry of distress. The lady dropped onto the chair with an exhausted exhale.

"Have you no further explanation? Have you nothing else to say for yourself?" Mama asked under her breath.

Atticus's jaw tightened. "I would not have you think that Felicity is at fault in any way. She is perfectly innocent and blameless."

"Then begin from the beginning," Papa prodded, his gaze more serious than Atticus had ever seen.

What good would there be in lying or masking the truth now? It was done. Mere information, unchangeable like the text on a page. Atticus shared it all—even Lady Swan and Felicity's lie by omission, understandable yet painful nonetheless. At some point as he spoke, Atticus had raised his head to meet his parents' commiserating gazes.

"Heavens above," Mama whispered when Atticus finished, her eyes wider than should have been possible.

"That…is certainly not what I expected to hear." Papa leaned back in his chair and stretched his neck side to side. "Breakfast is not yet finished and I already require a nap."

"As do I," Atticus admitted. Every limb hung heavy with an exhaustion that transcended the physical. It penetrated his very spirit.

"So you see, all this time, I thought we had found each other by some miracle. That Felicity had found something in me worthy of being fully loved and understood and entrusted. In reality, she was being guided by this letter, the orchestrator of our fates, and I would have been none the wiser had Miss Clara not forgotten that I was never meant to know. The situation has become so increasingly entangled that it is now impossible to know which threads lead to truth and which only give the appearance of it, ending instead in knots of confusion."

Mama frowned. "I do not agree."

"I fail to see on what grounds." Atticus shook his head and crushed the napkin in his fist. Surely, even his naturally optimistic mama would not attempt to find a positive outcome in this mess.

"It is quite simple. Do you love your wife?"

Atticus fought to keep from grimacing. "It is not that simple."

"Very well, perhaps not. The question is still relevant. Do you *love* your wife?"

"Yes. Of course I do."

Mama and Papa exchanged a knowing glance that Atticus was not sure if he should like or not. He swallowed the anxious lump in his throat.

"We know you do, son," Mama continued. Papa took her hand as if in silent endorsement. "And we know Felicity loves you. We know you bring each other immense happiness. That is all. That *is* the truth."

The listless remains of Atticus's heart stirred in his chest. How desperately he longed to believe her! He was so desperate, in fact, that he did believe it for half a beat.

"But how? How are we to overcome all that has tainted our

marriage since before we met? How can we truly know if what we feel now will remain forever, because it is true...or if it will wither, because the soil in which it was planted was never meant to sustain it? What if one day, Felicity realizes that her feelings and the intrigue of the letter have faded with time, and that she was right to call us a mistake? How long will it take for her to inform me of that development?"

There was that strange sideways look again. Atticus narrowed his eyes. Apparently, there was still more to be said, but this time, not by him.

"Atticus, you know your mother and I love each other very much," Papa began slowly. Atticus nodded, knots coiling in his stomach. "But...there was a time in our lives when your mother and I, in fact, loathed each other."

All of Atticus's propriety and good breeding disappeared in an instant. His mouth dropped open.

"Pardon?" he demanded. His bulging eyes bounced back and forth between the older couple's sheepish smiles.

"We were both young and had only just been introduced when I overheard your papa, in a foolish attempt to impress his haughty classmates from Oxford, insult my dearest friend at the time," Mama continued with a giggle, her entire countenance aglow with the memory of her youth. "Something about all the turquoise feathers in her hair failing to distract from her plainness, both in features and in manners."

Atticus's mouth fell open as he stared at his father, who offered a sheepish shrug.

"Your mama made certain I—and all my classmates—knew precisely how she felt about my comment," said Papa. "I was young and foolish indeed. Though might I add, that friend whom your mama defended so gallantly on that fateful evening has not returned any of her correspondence in nearly twenty years."

Atticus sank back into his chair, his long arms dangling over the sides. Mama and Papa were too enamored with their reminiscences to mind.

"And so you...*loathed* each other? I cannot imagine it."

The older woman chuckled, turning her fond smile from her husband to her son.

"That is just the thing, Atticus. Even we can hardly imagine it ourselves now. We have spent so much more of our lives loving each other that our origins, crucial to our love story though they are, carry so much less significance when weighed against the decades of joy we have shared since."

Papa did not remove his soft gaze from his wife as he effortlessly continued her thought. "Eventually, after weeks of inadvertently crossing paths throughout London and renewing our bitter vows of lifelong hatred at every turn, we began to realize that we were actually being drawn to each other. We shared a lengthy conversation and apologies on both sides—after which, I apologized to your mama's friend—and began a courtship much like many others. What once seemed impossible is now a distant memory we reflect upon with gratitude and amusement."

Atticus continued to stare in wonder at the neat abridgment of this aspect of his parents' pasts. It had been completely unknown to him, and no doubt Arabella as well.

"But," he began, struggling to formulate a sensible rebuttal while also absorbing this new information.

"We know our situation and yours are not exactly comparable," Mama continued, "but perhaps we might be taken as proof that strange, even undesirable, conditions need not rob you of an entire future of happiness. When you are living these days as they happen, every shift brings a new frustration that seems insurmountable. But if you persevere now, you and Felicity shall create so many memories of far greater importance that all of this business of Lady Swan and secrets and scandals will grow small in the distance."

Atticus sat in pensive silence for several long moments. It sounded so simple, just as they had said. It sounded so tempting.

All these new dreams he had finally allowed himself to dream could be his if only he and Felicity could set aside their past.

Finally, Atticus forced himself to speak. "Thank you very much, Mama, Papa. You have given me much to consider and much for both of us to discuss."

"We will keep you in our prayers, darling," Mama cooed. The hope in her eyes returned as she stood.

"You will overcome this. We know it. You look as though you require some time to think, so we shall grant it," offered Papa, also rising from his chair.

Atticus accepted a few more reassurances as well as a breathtaking hug from Mama and returned to his quiet reflection. His spirits sank to depths lower than he'd thought possible. What else had he done but delayed his parents' disappointment yet again? It would become clear all too soon that Atticus had irrevocably failed. Felicity had made her decision and Atticus had not had the strength to fight her. He was still not sure the happiness of which his parents had spoken with such reverence could be possible for him and his wife.

But they had not seen the way she had looked at him. They did not know her as he did. As he'd thought he did.

After some untold amount of time, sitting and staring at the empty chair to his right, Atticus felt his body stir of its own accord. His legs forced him up and to the door, down the hall, up the stairs, and into his library. As if his body understood what his mind could not dictate, what his mind needed: the solitude of his sanctuary.

Atticus's distracted mind came into sharp focus as he approached the corner. Their corner. What had once belonged to Atticus alone now bore painful reminders of another, not only in the items she had left behind—her book, a pair of gloves, a tea-stained shawl—but in the very air of the room.

He squeezed his eyes shut and inhaled deeply. Did traces of her perfume linger? Or did he simply imagine it to stave off the inevitable cascade of loss waiting to crush him the moment he lowered his defenses?

Perhaps it had been a mistake to invite Felicity into this particular aspect of his life. It would never be the same now that she'd touched it.

Atticus opened his eyes. At least he could set aside her items for her lady's maid to collect later. He steeled himself for the sting of handling the very same precious objects Felicity had held not long ago, but only came as far as the first.

He picked up the adventure novel Felicity had been reading these past few weeks. Atticus turned it over in his hands, pressing his palms to the leather covers. He hoped, even if she did not continue to read with him, that she would continue all the same. Eventually, most likely in the spring after a little warmth returned to the world, he might resume his new habit of outdoor walks...without his wife on his arm.

Together under the same roof, sharing a life, yet completely alone. That was the fate to which Atticus had unknowingly doomed them both, pulled along like a puppet on strings only his wife and this mysterious writer could see.

The harsh grip of misery crushed Atticus's chest. It nearly brought him to his knees. Instead, he found his favorite chair and leaned as deep into its protective wings as possible, Felicity's book still in his hands.

Atticus hesitated briefly before choosing self-indulgence. Here in this quiet corner, he might allow a moment to pity himself. No one would know. Least of all Felicity. She need not carry the burden of Atticus's pain.

No one would know if he raised the book to his face to steal another lungful of her familiar, sharp scent, as if it he might bottle it in his heart and tuck it into a corner that would fall deeper and deeper into darkness, if only so Atticus could remind himself on rare occasions of the three most glorious months of his life.

A moment was all it could be, Atticus soon reminded himself. He had already been granted far more of them than he deserved. In some ways, he had Lady Swan to thank as much as to blame for it.

As he rose to return the volume to the rest of Felicity's belongings, the pages fell open. Cursing his carelessness, Atticus caught the bookmark as it fluttered in elegant loops toward the ground and slipped it back into its rightful place.

His fingers brushed against a raised, irregular edge. A wax seal. The very blood in his veins froze.

It could not be. The chances were far too slim. His wife, though not a terribly popular correspondent by her own admission, received mail several times a week. It could be any letter.

If it were any letter, why had Felicity tried to hide it from him that day in library when she had returned home with Mrs. Harrowsmith's happy news?

Atticus shook his head. His grip tightened around the spine, his knuckles white. Even as guilt ravaged Atticus's insides, he raised his finger off the seal.

A purple swan. Just as Felicity had described.

And she had kept it right here in their place, in every book she had read beside Atticus. He recognized the one corner she often left peeking through the pages. It had been crushed one day when she'd dropped her book on the wooden floor. Surely, that must have accounted for something.

Atticus's temptation was too great to spend any further time pondering Felicity's intentions in using Lady Swan's letter as a bookmark. He flipped the sheet open.

"Perhaps you find it difficult to recognize love because you are so accustomed to being shown time and again that you are not worthy of it."

That line continued to swim before his eyes even after what must have been his fourth or fifth reading. It seeped into his bones, into his very soul, underscoring all the wisdom his parents had shared and everything his wife had confided in him. They converged into a sudden and stunning clarity in Atticus's mind.

Bold, brave Felicity was afraid. She was afraid to be a wife and mother because she did not think herself worthy of accepting such roles. She was afraid to love Atticus now because she had been made to feel unworthy of love for the entirety of her life.

Hand trembling, Atticus nestled the letter back into the book and shut it with a quiet *thump*.

That was what he had seen on her face last night. Fear. That was why his heart had longed to accept his parents' assurance that they truly could make each other happy if given a proper chance.

Lady Swan, whoever she was, had known it all along. Felicity lived in fear of what she believed she did not deserve.

Did that mean she believed she did not deserve Atticus when the opposite could not be more obvious?

This time when Atticus steeled himself, he did it with a confidence that had no place in a coward's heart like his. Yet it anchored him to solid, steady ground, his spine straight and head held high. He set Felicity's book down where he'd found it, on the red, velvet cushion of her chair.

Only time would tell if she would ever rejoin him in their domestic bliss. That was not his primary concern. As Atticus strode through the library, a strange silence settling over his plague of nerves, he knew one thing to be true.

It no longer mattered to him if Felicity could not bring herself to take this great risk and build their great reward hand in hand with him. That was a choice she must be free to make, now more than ever.

There was only one thing left for him to do, the thing Felicity needed above all else.

Atticus burst through the library doors. The footman at the end of the hall whirled around and hastily bowed.

"Where is Mrs. Wheadon? My Mrs. Wheadon?"

The older man glanced down at his glossy shoes. "I am afraid she is not at home, sir. She has not been since last night."

CHAPTER EIGHTEEN

"I AM NOT sure you should return just yet, Felicity," Mercy mumbled, head lowered.

Felicity wrapped her arms around her twin once more, her shawl protecting them both from the chill breeze seeping into Huxley's foyer from the open front doors. "I must. Setherwell is my home now. Wherever Atticus goes is my home—even if it will never again have the true comfort of home. I might as well accustom myself to the change now. I no longer have energy to run away from what must be."

"Sister," Mercy sniffled, her eyes red with sleeplessness and despondence. "I cannot bear to see you like this...without your light and your obstinate plans and your lively laugh. Are you certain there is nothing to be done? Surely, it is clear by now that Atticus is not the type of man to hate his wife over such a thing."

"I am certain," Felicity said in a rush. "Do not pity me, dear Mercy. The damage I have done deserves no sympathy or kindness. I must face the consequences of my terrible mistake. Besides, I would rather not let the viscountess know I was here. The chance of my discovery increases the closer her waking hour approaches."

With a reluctant frown, Mercy nodded. She released Felicity from her embrace and grasped both her hands. "I pray you will come to forgive yourself one day. As ignorant and cruel as you feel you have been, nothing you have done is worth a lifetime of inner torment. I believe, even if he wishes to avoid you forever, your husband would agree. Of that, I am very much certain."

Felicity forced a tight smile, her cheeks aching with the effort. "Thank you, sweet sister. It brings me relief to know I will always have a supporter in you, no matter how undeserving I may be. I do love and adore you, Mercy."

"And I love and adore you, even when you vex me so." Mercy chuckled, waving a hand at her watery, weary eyes.

A sliver of comfort did return to Felicity. Fondness softened her smile. "That is for the best, for I am afraid ours is a bond of particular steadfastness. You are the only person in this world who can never truly be rid of me."

"Thank goodness for that." Mercy grasped one of Felicity's hands in both of hers and brought it up to her face. "I shudder to think how dull and cold my life would have been had we come into this world separately. It is a shame not everyone is afforded the opportunity to share a soul with their very best friend since before birth."

"Miss Reeve! Mrs. Wheadon!" came an urgent whisper from somewhere behind the sisters. They turned to find Mercy's lady's maid hurrying down the grand staircase. "Her ladyship stirs," she announced in a breathless huff halfway down.

"I must go. Thank you, my darling, dearest Mercy," Felicity repeated, squeezing her twin yet again before flying to the door.

A biting gust whipped about her as she charged across the lawn to the treeline. She pulled her muslin shawl tighter about her and nearly regretted sending the carriage she had taken last night back to Setherwell.

Felicity tried and failed to focus on her steady, forceful march the closer she came to the familiar shadow in the branches, the path that had so unexpectedly led her to the greatest joy she had ever experienced—and the cruelest pain, entirely self-inflicted. Eyes fixed on that spot, Felicity's frantic, rebellious heart flooded her senses with that memory, as if she might transport herself back in time to this very moment on a bright, summer day, ignorant to all that awaited her.

Tears stung Felicity's eyes. If by some miracle she could return to that wonderful, terrible day that had changed her life—her very being—would she choose differently? Would she fall wholeheartedly and honestly and never look back?

To go back in time would be her only hope of reversing this terrible predicament. No matter how deeply she felt the pain of regret, no matter how ardently she apologized, she knew she could never expect Atticus to entrust his heart to her again. In her panic, she had been careless with it.

Or would Felicity still have made the same mistakes that had led both of them to their present misery?

She would never know. It was foolish to speculate on what could not be changed, Felicity reminded herself as she ducked between the protection of the trees. The wind died to a haunting whistle. She was nearly back to the street that would lead her to Setherwell. It was time to brace herself for whatever fresh sorrows the day brought.

Felicity shook her head. Leaves crumpled softly under her feet against the packed dirt path. She did not wish to think upon the future, either.

Would she see Atticus at all today? Tomorrow? For the remainder of their time in Bainbridge? When they did inevitably cross paths, would his stunning, blue eyes look at her with icy indifference or subdued hatred? Or would they simply look right through her?

The torrent of questions that populated Felicity's mind refused to be banished, no matter how hard she blinked or shook her head or swatted through the air. It was a unique sort of torment, to know she would never be the same in the eyes of someone she had come to understand and admire and...love.

"Ah!" she cried, jerking back and nearly losing her balance.

Felicity spun around and grabbed hold of her shawl, snagged against a prickly bunch of naked branches. Naturally, just the thing she needed in her time of distress.

With an impatient growl, Felicity tugged. The branches swayed under the force of her pull. They did not snap or relinquish the delicate fabric. Felicity gritted her teeth and yanked again.

The rustle of leaves and branches echoed behind her as something large crashed down the narrow path. Pulse quickening, Felicity pulled with all her desperate might, not daring so much as a glance over her shoulder to see what wild animal or vagabond charged at her.

"Felicity!"

She stilled. Her heart slowed, stumbled, wilted. So soon? Felicity had been relying on at least a few more minutes to compose herself. Tense fingers loosened around the torn fabric.

"Atticus. I did not mean to trouble you into coming after me," Felicity replied without turning.

"It is never any trouble."

His boots whispered over fallen leaves, making almost no sound as he approached, so different from the urgent commotion of moments before. Felicity could not help being acutely aware of every movement, no matter how quiet.

"You mustn't say such things anymore," Felicity mumbled, not entirely sure she meant for him to hear.

Atticus's steps stopped just behind her. Two long arms enclosed Felicity, reaching past her head. The mixture of his proximity and enticing aroma made her knees weaken as he made quick work of untangling her shawl.

He could not continue doing such things anymore. How could Felicity ever hope to regain even a shred of peace in her heartache if Atticus continued to remind her of her grave error and the suffering she'd caused with every gentle word and consideration?

"Why mustn't I say such things anymore?" he asked as he stepped back and turned Felicity by her shoulders, wrapping the thin fabric about her in the process.

She stared at her husband. He had given her no choice. Felicity's heart shot into her throat as she failed to read his solemn expression.

"Because you waste your kindness. Because it is not necessary any longer," she whispered, almost pleading. How much longer could she bear to look into those same eyes that had been so filled with anguish last night?

"I say them because—"

"Because it will always be your duty to me as your wife—"

"Because I love you."

Felicity stilled once more. The wind faded. The chill melted into sweet, sheltering warmth. Just for a moment, she allowed herself to feel it. This may be the only time she ever heard those words from her husband.

Atticus's fingers slipped past the layers of Felicity's shawl until they found her hands and wrapped around them. Without her permission, Felicity's eyes closed. Her skin responded, soaking in his welcome heat.

This should not have been happening. Then why did it feel *so* perfect? Why did it feel like coming home?

"I did not exaggerate when I told you that I have spent the majority of my life believing I would never love anyone. And to discover I could love someone this completely, this quickly... It defies everything I knew about myself."

"Felicity, you opened my eyes to all that I might be, to all the wonders I might find if I am not afraid to look. Once opened, they can never be shut again. I am incapable of returning to who I was before you brought your light into my life. And even if I were capable, I should not wish to. For that, I will be eternally grateful."

Shaking her head, Felicity stepped back. "I am sorry, truly. I never intended for it to happen."

Atticus took the same step, never releasing Felicity's hands. His grip remained light. She knew she could pull at any moment, but she was far too weak. This must have been a dream. Why else did she see nothing but that captivating, blue gaze?

"If the restrictions you set forth last night are still what you desire, I will derive my happiness in abiding by them until my last breath. On that account, you must not spare a single thought for my perceived troubles.

"My greatest wish, my only wish, is for you to find whatever comfort possible in this entanglement. To that end, I have already informed my parents of my intention to purchase Setherwell, that you might always be near your sister and friends. I will not consign you to decades of loneliness. Perhaps Mercy may come live with us at Setherwell, or wherever we reside, so she need not remain victim to loneliness, either."

As Atticus spoke, Felicity's mouth fell open, her eyes filling with tears. She snatched her hands away and stumbled back into a sturdy tree trunk. The gentleman flinched in surprise.

"But why?" Felicity demanded through the stinging crack in her voice. "Why—after what I hid from you, after robbing your life of its plans, after all this uncertainty that has plagued us since the beginning…after what I said—how can you still be so kind?"

Though his focus never left Felicity, Atticus remained grounded to his spot, allowing her the distance she'd thought she'd needed. Instead, Felicity felt his loss more keenly even than last night, when she had been so sure that the only way to spare them future pain was to break their hearts now.

"Because I no longer care. Not about Lady Swan. Our scandalous engagement. Worries that may never come to pass."

Felicity could not continue to witness the earnest desire in her husband's face, clinging to the illusion they had unwittingly woven. "You can never be certain of anything I say. I misled you. I hurt you…"

"Felicity." The quiet confidence in his voice compelled her to raise her head. Atticus's gaze drew her toward him, as if the physical distance meant nothing to their hearts when they still shared this unspoken language.

"I am telling you, once and for all, that I love you *now*. Secrets or not. Falling in love with you, every part of you, was real. Every moment we shared was genuine. Nothing else matters to me. I know my mind in this."

The tall, lean figure of her husband blurred as more tears flooded Felicity's vision, on the precipice of spilling. "How can such a thing be possible?"

"Because it is what you deserve."

A tear slipped out before Felicity could take herself in hand. She longed to free them. She longed to free herself in the mad hope that she could accept what she so desperately desired.

Atticus came closer, even closer than before. They stood toe to toe. Felicity could no longer resist, not with him a mere breath away. Her gloved fingers found his, tentative. "I still do not understand... Perhaps I never will."

"You will." Atticus's voice rang with conviction as he intertwined their hands. "If permitted, I will never tire of telling you and showing you in every way I can imagine that you deserve all the love and care your guardians failed to provide. You deserve to know it and feel it every second of every day—whether you return my affections or not."

He paused. For the first time, his gaze faltered. Felicity could hardly believe her ears. But her heart did. It sputtered back to life.

Despite all her rashness and stubbornness, her husband loved her. He wanted her. He accepted her. Simply because Felicity was Felicity. Never had such a rush of sweet, perfect contentment threatened to sweep her off her feet.

"But before you take anything else into consideration, I have another confession... I read the letter you keep in your book."

Felicity's surprise only lasted a moment. "I suppose you would be curious. Apparently, Clara confessed that she spoke of Lady Swan with you to Mercy in tears after they departed Setherwell last night, the poor thing."

"I do apologize, truly," Atticus hurried without meeting her gaze. "It was a moment of weakness, one that will not be repeated again under any circumstances. But, if I may give credit where it is due..."

A weak chuckle grew into a giggle which became a full, free laugh. When Felicity's once-mournful tears spilled, they left behind them a tingle of unexpected elation. Atticus's grip tightened around her hand as he joined.

"While I will always hate being bested, I will admit that Lady Swan possesses a remarkable talent with words—and perhaps the gift of foresight." Felicity gasped as their amusement slowly settled. "But, Atticus..." She lowered her gaze.

With a gentle finger, Atticus tilted Felicity's chin up. Her eyes lifted and found his. "Yes?"

"The regret that has plagued me since the moment those words left my mouth is indescribable. Even a talent such as Shakespeare could have never hoped to capture it...although he came remarkably close."

Her husband chuckled quietly as his forefinger drifted along her jaw. His soft palm cupped her cheek.

"I knew, the very instant I said it, that it was a dreadful error to call our marriage a mistake, yet I had somehow convinced myself it was right. Being near me has clearly been nothing but a hazard to you. The amount of pain I have caused you since the night of the ball—"

"Is a mere drop in the sea of elation you have brought me in that very same time."

Felicity turned her face into his touch. "I am so, so terribly sorry, Atticus. For everything, for not coming forth with the letter. But most particularly for choosing cowardice last night. I wish I had not waited to lose you to accept that running from one's misdeeds and faults tends to create more problems than it solves.

"Lady Swan opened me to the possibility that I could let myself be vulnerable in the process of falling in love—even if I never would have admitted it then. But I have come to believe that, if we had met in an entirely ordinary fashion, your very essence would have eventually drawn me to you. I have never known anyone as sweet, caring, understanding, or fascinating as you. I like to think that I would have recognized that on my own had Lady Swan not intervened, though I am sure it would have taken far, far longer."

"Your love for me is…genuine?" Atticus whispered, his lips brushing against her forehead.

"It is unbearably genuine."

"And does this mean you wish to live permanently at Sether-well?"

There was that darling hint of bashfulness that Felicity had come to cherish. She freed her hands and allowed them to wander up his strong forearms and biceps to his shoulders…his neck. Her fingers teased at his tangled locks.

"It means I wish to live permanently with *you*, Atticus. As your wife, in the deepest, truest sense. But only if you are certain you can accept me after—"

Atticus's arms tightened around Felicity's waist. He smiled and lowered his head ever so slightly. "It has very recently been brought to my attention that we both have already lost far too much time needlessly denying ourselves."

"I think I finally agree," Felicity whispered. "I love you, Atticus. I have always known it, but my fear of changing who I was and still finding myself unworthy of you distorted even the most natural truth."

"My kind, vibrant, beautiful wife."

"My brave, unwavering, dashing husband."

Felicity tilted her face up just as Atticus brought his head lower. Their foreheads collided with a surprisingly resonant smack, their wide eyes mirroring each other's shock.

The couple let their heads fall back as they released bellows of delight in unison. Felicity gasped for breath, freeing a hand to block the no doubt ghastly sight from her husband's view.

Instead, he caught it and returned it to its comfortable position cupping the back of his neck. For some reason, the deftness of his movements, usually so deliberate and cautious, flushed Felicity with heat.

"Your laugh is the true thing that brought us into each other's lives. Never bury it."

"You may come to regret that," Felicity teased with a shrug.

"Impossible. Now let me see what damage has been done."

Atticus's free hand grasped Felicity's jaw while the other pulled her closer. He pressed his lips to her forehead, banishing her pain and guilt and regret.

"I love you so very, very much, Felicity."

Felicity felt the loss of his warm mouth only for a moment. He captured her lips and held her for a wonderfully timeless moment. They savored each other, explored each other with slow, gentle movements.

Exhilaration erupted in Felicity's chest like a flock of doves taking to endless skies. Her fingers twisted into his hair as his hand drew her face even closer, each increasingly desperate for the other.

How many times had she tried and failed to stop herself from imagining this wonderful moment of their first true kiss? None of those vague dreams could have prepared her for how completely Atticus's very being enveloped her. He was all she could see, hear, feel, taste.

Time held no meaning for them in the tunnel of trees. Time would never be the same for Felicity now that she could see all their future blessings unfolding before them, wrapped in the tender promise of her husband's kiss.

There still existed the part of her that refused to believe she deserved to love someone as selfless and perfect as Atticus.

But this feeling...this indescribable, otherworldly feeling as Atticus nestled her face into the warm crook of his neck and held her tight refused to be silenced any longer.

It outweighed all else. This feeling of rightness. It was so simple, Felicity had almost missed it.

"Are you ready to return home?" Atticus whispered into her hair.

"But you make such a lovely shawl, much better than this

muslin thing. Still, I suppose you must be chilled to the bone. You despise the cold."

Felicity burrowed a little deeper into her husband's embrace and rested her ear over his heart. It beat strong and steady. It beat for her.

"I do not despise it, not entirely. Not with you. But I am afraid I shall have to take matters into my own hands," Atticus replied slowly, a touch of mischief coloring his words. Felicity's eyes narrowed.

"And how do you plan on—"

Her teasing question was swallowed by a shocked squeal as Atticus hoisted her with little effort into his arms. Every inch of her skin ablaze, Felicity stared into those eyes she loved so dearly, eyes she would lose herself in every day for the remainder of her life.

In less than a heartbeat, Atticus's sweet lips found hers once more. Felicity melted in his strong arms, weightless.

"What an uncommon man." She sighed, utterly content. "You surprise me at every turn."

"Thanks to my bride, I have grown quite fond of surprises." Atticus chuckled.

Felicity felt the lovely sound echo through her own body and soul as if it had generated within her. They had been one for far longer than she'd realized.

They had been one all along.

EPILOGUE

"**G**OOD MORNING, MY love."

Atticus's familiar, sleepy voice drifted through the dressing room. His soft footsteps approached behind Felicity. She did not turn. She did not remove her eyes from the mirror or her hands from her middle.

"Are you quite well, Felicity?" Atticus prodded as his reflection joined hers in the glass. His hands settled upon her shoulders. "It is a rare day that you rise before I do."

Felicity inhaled a shuddering breath as she continued to examine herself. Her fingers curled into the soft fabric of her nightgown. Nothing looked different, yet she had never felt stranger. In the mirror, Felicity's eyes drifted up to meet Atticus's.

"Darling?" Ever so gently, Atticus turned Felicity to face him and grasped her face in both hands. "You do look frightfully pale. And yet no fever?"

"I awoke in the early hours. My stomach was in such a state. I snuck out the chamber pot and called for Hammond to assist me in my old quarters so as not to disturb you."

Alarm flooded Atticus's face. "Heavens, my poor wife! We must send for the physician at once!"

"Not yet," Felicity insisted with a muffled chuckle.

Just like that, the terror that had been coursing through her veins—and turning her stomach out into her chamber pot—evaporated. Not completely, to be sure, but enough to free

Felicity to relish the moment, a skill she had been diligently developing with Atticus's support.

What had she to fear with this man by her side?

"B-But, darling, we must act quickly, lest your ailment return or worsen. And please, whatever troubles you, you must promise to wake or fetch me in the future, I care not for the hour—"

"I wanted to be certain first—quite certain—before I said a word to you."

The line between Atticus's thick brows deepened. He clung to her, desperate. "You know you are at liberty to share anything with me at any time—"

Atticus's anxious rambling fell away the moment Felicity pressed the palm of his hand to her stomach. "Felicity?"

Emotion squeezed Felicity's chest at the hesitant hopefulness in her beloved husband's voice. "Atticus…"

"Are you…? Are we…?"

"I am. We are."

Atticus grasped the back of Felicity's head and kissed her as if all his dreams had just come true. Draping her arms across his broad shoulders, Felicity kissed him back with the very same passion. She knew hers certainly had.

"A baby." Atticus gasped when they finally pulled apart for air. Tears glittered in the eyes Felicity prayed their little one would inherit. "Perhaps he or she will arrive in time to enjoy the strawberries and cornflowers with us."

"You are to be a father," Felicity announced in a deliriously gleeful giggle.

Trailing his knuckles across Felicity's skin, Atticus tucked a loose lock behind her ear. "And you are to be a wonderful mother."

Felicity bristled against the pinprick of doubt in the back of her mind. It had demanded her attention with decreasing frequency as she and Atticus had fully embraced this new chapter of their married life…until three months ago, when her suspicions had first begun. As she had said, she'd needed to be *quite* sure.

"You believe so?"

Atticus kissed Felicity's forehead and left his lips there for several long breaths before answering. "I have never had a moment's doubt. In fact, I am surprised you still doubt yourself. Look at you."

Taking Felicity's hand, Atticus turned her back to the mirror. They stood side by side, Felicity still in her cap and robe, Atticus still sporting his morning jacket and slippers and daily mop of tangled hair.

"Look at you," Atticus repeated. "You are radiant with happiness. Such happiness could not exist without great desire and great love."

This time, Felicity looked not at her unremarkable stomach, but at her face. Into her own eyes. She smiled. She saw it—the radiant happiness Atticus had brought into her life. And now it had made another life.

"It is entirely thanks to you," she whispered, reaching up to cup her husband's cheek. "Whatever lies ahead, whatever past or future fears we find ourselves facing, we are never alone in them."

"Even more so now," Atticus added as he returned his hand to Felicity's middle. "We will always support each other. All of us. Exactly as we are. I love you so very, very much."

"I love you, too, darling Atticus. And I pray that means you will support my idea."

Atticus peered down into Felicity's face. "Anything. Name it and it is yours. My life's mission from this moment forward is to dote upon you and fulfill your every whim."

Warmth prickled under Felicity's skin. "You do that already, and magnificently, I might add."

"Ah, tonight's dinner. Do you wish to cancel? You know I will never be opposed to canceling."

Felicity chuckled and shook her head. "No, as a matter of fact, the dinner happens to be perfectly timed. But about the impending Season…"

Several hours later, Felicity and Atticus stood in the center of Setherwell's drawing room, every curious eye upon them. Felicity tucked her hand into Atticus's, relaxing his anxious fist.

"Thank you all for joining us tonight," she began, forcing herself not to rush through the words. "Though this was not the original intent for the evening, we thought this a fine opportunity to make an announcement to our dearest ones."

The companionable stillness in the room shifted. It became heavy with anticipation. Only Mercy and Mr. and Mrs. Wheadon did not appear perplexed.

Felicity fought a grin as Clara perched on the very edge of her seat, Ellen pinching the back of her bodice as if to keep her younger sister from flying away. Lydia, absentmindedly rubbing circles over her stomach—which looked fit to burst any day now—and Isabel exchanged suspicious glances while Sebastian remained primarily focused on massaging his wife's shoulders, a favorite activity of hers as she neared her own special arrival.

Their families wore politely confused expressions and whispered amongst each other while glancing to Mr. and Mrs. Wheadon by the fireplace for any hints. The older couple clutched each other's hands, barely containing the excitement of the secret knowledge they, along with Mercy, had gained during breakfast. Lord and Lady Eldmar, who had decided to begin their Season early, would learn of it in a letter.

"Atticus and I will not be accompanying you all to London this year."

Their guests deflated.

"Come now, dear wife, do not keep them in suspense," said Atticus in an intentionally loud whisper.

When Felicity looked up at her husband, she found him smiling down at her with a lovely mixture of fondness and mischief. She lost the battle with her own grin and looked out at her new mother and father, her sister, and her beloved friends and neighbors.

"We will not be joining for very good reason, I assure you. The long journey will aggravate this one, I am afraid."

Felicity patted her abdomen and marveled once more that in several months, she would be as round as Lydia. The drawing room erupted in gasps, which transformed into cheers and claps. Five young ladies raced toward them.

Before they knew it, the couple found themselves wrapped in an embrace of seemingly countless arms. At the center of the mad celebration, their laughter rang the loudest.

"Come, Atticus. I believe I have some words of wisdom to share with you from my recent experience of maintaining a wife's happiness during this delicate time," announced Sebastian as he dutifully followed after Lydia with a sympathetic smile.

"Oh, thank goodness." Atticus sighed with relief. He hurried after his friend, wringing his hands. The poor fellow's anxiety had come and gone in waves all day. But his sheer joy and excitement had been constant.

"How absolutely wonderful, Felicity!" Ellen whimpered before turning away to wipe her button nose.

"Congratulations to you both." Lydia gasped as she patted Ellen's back.

The larger her belly had grown, the more difficult it had become for her to inhale a full breath. Felicity was grateful that Lydia had embarked on this adventure before her. She already had a dozen questions about what was to come and what was already happening—such as when the aroma of freshly cooked eggs would become welcome to her once more.

"Two babies! We are to have two babies in Bainbridge!" cheered Clara as she dreamily spun about their group, earning chuckles from the other guests. "Perhaps more, if Lady Swan's successes continue," she added in a half-whisper, half-giggle behind a gloved hand.

"Now, Clara, you are getting quite ahead of yourself. Allow us to celebrate Felicity's blessing first." Isabel laughed, one arm around Felicity's waist.

"A blessing, indeed," said Mercy from Felicity's other side. Her voice quavered, tears in her eyes. Felicity extracted herself from Isabel and walked a few steps away from the others with her twin.

"I simply cannot wait to spoil my precious niece or nephew," Mercy continued. "I am so, so pleased for you, dearest Felicity."

"This child will never know what it is to be without love," she replied around the lump in her throat. Heavens, she was so prone to fits of weeping these days!

Mercy reached up and touched the corner of Felicity's eye with a gloved finger. "You and Atticus will make certain of that."

Felicity nodded and glanced over her shoulder at her husband, who diligently scribbled Sebastian's advice into the notebook he kept in his pocket. "We certainly will."

After another few hours of food and merry conversation, the exhaustion of pure happiness settled into Felicity's bones. She did adore hosting, yet it could be taxing even without the additional responsibility of growing their child within.

"Let us rest, my loves." Atticus sighed as he guided Felicity out of the drawing room with one arm around her shoulders. "You do promise to wake me should you feel unwell, yes?"

"I promise, dear Atticus." Felicity chuckled and rested her head against her husband's shoulder.

"Madam!"

The pair paused and turned. The butler rushed toward them from the stairs, something in his hand.

"Another odd occurrence, madam. It was left on the doorstep yet again, addressed to you."

Felicity and Atticus smiled at each other as she accepted the letter. "Thank you, Lambert. There is no need for concern."

As he bowed and retreated, they turned their attention to the purple seal.

"Strange how this familiar swan inspires such feelings of gratitude in me now when, months ago, the sight of it filled me with dread."

"I am forever grateful that you decided to open her first letter," Atticus whispered as he came around behind Felicity and wrapped his arms around her middle, not too tightly.

"I suspect she has had word of our news, but how? How can it be possible if only a select few knew until just a few hours ago?" Felicity mused, her mind catching onto the thought. "Could Lady Swan have been among them, after all? Still, I suppose servants may have already gossiped—"

Atticus chuckled, his chest firm against her back. "Perhaps, my dear, some mysteries are best enjoyed when they remain unsolved."

Remembering herself, as if eager for word from an old friend, Felicity snapped the seal open and read aloud, Atticus's chin resting on her shoulder.

"Dearest Mrs. Atticus Wheadon, it has come to this writer's attention that a most hearty congratulations are in order! Nothing brings a champion of romance greater joy than to welcome another generation raised in a foundation of the deepest love, as you and your sweet husband clearly share.

"Your individual challenges, though different in many ways, shaped who you must become in order to find and heal each other. Together, no matter the circumstances, you achieve balance and peace—the unsung gifts of true love. Thank you both for seeing past fear to the wonders waiting beyond. Your hearts will lead you now to more beautiful dreams you can yet imagine.

"Yours Always, Lady Swan."

About the Author

Penny Fairbanks has been a voracious reader since she could hold a book and immediately fell in love with Jane Austen and her world. Now Penny has branched out into writing her own romantic tales.

Penny lives in the Midwest with her charming husband and their aptly named cat, Prince. When she's not writing or reading, she enjoys drinking a lot of coffee and rewatching The Office.

Come follow me on Facebook to stay up to date on my latest news and coming releases.

facebook.com/pennyfairbanksauthor